Suggestion

Nigel White

*For Mo
Best Wishes
Nigel White*

ISBN 978-1-8380634-5-0

First published in Great Britain: September 2020
by www.sugarcubepublishing.co.uk

Front Cover:
"Butterfly Meadow" by Eleanor Belton

Frontispiece:
"Bluebell Wood" by Cathy Fox

Printed and Bound in Great Britain by
Sarsen Press, 22 Hyde Street, Winchester, Hampshire SO23 7DR

THE MORAL RIGHT OF THE AUTHOR HAS BEEN ASSERTED

Thankyou. I would like to thank Mrs Joan Lush for her advice on farming matters, and Mr George Hofman for his thoughts on antique furniture construction.

By the same author:

"get Him out"   published 2017

" .... watching people cry".   published 2018

DEDICATION

For Alison
The very best 'Best Lady'

She lifted the infant from it's crib, parted her blouse, and began to nurse.

"You ask what I'd be", she said. She cradled the child .... and smiled.

"I'd be a pirate's doxy", she said. "That's what I'd be. Tight bodices and long skirts. Bare feet on wet decks. The bottom of my petticoats sodden and salt stained. Having to pee in a bucket. Dirty hair .... and grubby sex. Swaying decks and Caribbean sun. Being told what to do, and beaten for it if I don't. But there would be him. A pirate. And there'd be my love for him .... and what he stood for. What he meant to me.

Yeah .... I'd be a pirate's doxy. That's what I'd be ....

From: "A Necklace of a Thousand Stars"

Used by permission

ONE

Nell glanced up from the table that she was scrubbing clean. She had heard a horse in the road outside the Inn. Had she had a companion in her labours, then her helpmate could scarce have but noticed that Nell's cheeks must betray the condition of her heart. On this occasion, however, Nell was to be disappointed. The young man tying his horse to a ring set in the front wall of the tavern, was Giles Barnes, a local farmer. Nell smiled, Giles was a pleasant enough customer, well known to herself and to her father. He farmed to the north of the village. A typical farm of the area, poultry in the farm yard, milking cattle in the valley pastures, sheep on the chalk downs, and (a recent addition by Giles himself), some fifteen acres of arable land under cultivation, showing a fine crop of oats to be harvested in late summer.

Nell smoothed her apron, and tidied back her hair, as Giles came into the tap room.

"Good afternoon Sir", she said, "Have you brought us a thirst that we might serve to quench".

"Nell", he said, "Such formality ..... when we used to play together in the village school ......".

"Yes", she said, " .... and a marvel that I am blessed with a head of hair, so often did you delight in pulling my tails".

Giles laughed.

"Did I indeed", he said, "Then it must have been for the sole purpose of attracting your sweet attentions dear Nell".

"Sweet attentions ....", she said. "Did I not crown you with my lunch pail on one occasion .... and I'm sure that you deserved no less a reward for your efforts to re-fashion my locks".

"I'm sure I deserved no less", smiled Giles, "But you are correct in your assumptions regarding my thirst. It is indeed a warm afternoon out there on the road, and I have ridden from market. This shady room, and a cool ale would be pleasant a respite".

Nell crossed the room, lifted Giles' pewter tankard from it's hook on the beam, and drew him off a quart from a barrel layed over with wet towels.

He had seated himself at the settle in the far corner.

"Are you wanting food", she asked, as she put the tankard before him.

He took a sip, sat back against the settle, and sighed with pleasure.

"A wonderful refreshment", he said, "But no Nell, to answer your question .... no food .... I shall eat when I return home".

"Have you then found somebody to provide for you", she asked in surprise. She knew that he was lately without family. She saw a shadow cross Giles' face. His father had died but two months since, gored to death in the yard by the farm bull.

"I'll fare well enough Nell", he said. "I have a large ham to carve from, and there is a new loaf in my saddle bag there outside".

Nell shook her head. To change the subject, she thought to his farm.

"How do your new arable fields suit you", she asked.

Giles smiled.

"Well enough", he said. "My father had foresight to send me as apprentice to a farm in Cambridgeshire. I had time enough there to study the cycle of growing Wheat, and Barley".

"But you have chosen to cultivate Oats", she said.

He laughed.

"Nell", he said. "Is there any news that does not travel via your taproom".

She shook her head.

"Precious little", she said. "But it is Oats that you are growing".

"It is", he said, "At the request of a brewer ..... so I have sold the grain before it has even swelled on the stalk".

"And your milk herd .... it fares well", she asked.

"Milking well", he said, " .... and so they should on that lush grass in the valley".

Nell went to pick up her brush and pail .... but Giles motioned her to tarry.

"Nell", he said. "You show a keen interest in affairs of agriculture".

Nell blushed.

"No more than any country person who cares for their bread and their butter", she replied.

Giles sipped again from his tankard. He seemed thoughtful.

"With such an interest", he said, "I am surprised you are not a farmer's wife".

The comment was made so casually, but Nell could not fail to notice that he watched with great interest for her reply.

And Nell knew that just a sentence here, a smile, perhaps the touch of a hand .... and she saw a bridal gown and a village Church, and a throng of local people, and a decorated cart, and she saw herself lifted across the threshold of the farm ....

She saw herself as the domestic head of a thriving enterprise. She saw security. The dairy to run. Poultry to manage. Summer in the corn fields. Harvest homes, and Christmas gatherings .... and children around her skirts.

She looked at Giles. He was a fine young man. And with a fine reputation for charity in her community. A widow without firewood would soon find faggots by her door. A mother without milk for a child would find a copper pail set on her kitchen table. If there was want, or need, and Giles had the means to answer it, he found a way. But never to seek recognition. The faggots, the milk, perhaps a pair of loaves would appear, but none ever saw the bringer.

Nell shook her head.

"Giles", she said, "I am far too young to be thinking of marriage. A farmer needs a virtuous and sensible hard working companion for his wife. Not an Inn keeper's daughter to make his life a trial".

Giles laughed.

"I believe a farmer might manage you and your ways", he said. "Perhaps you should prepare yourself for such a proposal .... were it ever to come your way".

He drained his ale. He stood, and bowed.

"You should think on these matters", he said.

He left the cool of the taproom, and Nell watched him through the window as he mounted, and set off through the village towards his farm.

She sighed. Her father came into the room. Nell suspected he had been listening beyond the door to the parlour.

"A fine young man", he said. "I knew his father. You could go further .... and fare much worse".

Nell crossed the room, and embraced him. He was hot from work in the store room.

"Shall I pour you an ale", she asked.

Her father held her at arm's length, looking at her. He kissed her forehead.

"Too early for me", he said, "but mind you do not let it grow too late to assign your heart, young lady.

He returned to his work, and Nell resumed her cleaning .... but she soon laid down her brush, and sank onto a chair by the chimney.

"Giles is a good man", she thought. "He would indeed be a good husband to me. He would be a good father. He has the respect of all who know him".

She closed her eyes.

"But suppose ....", she thought. " .... suppose I were to tell Giles where I was last night. What might he think of me then ....".

TWO

As the last customer left the tap room of the Ship Inn .... it had proved to be a surprisingly busy evening .... Nell began to extinguish the candles spread around the room. She glanced towards her father who was washing the pewter tankards, and hanging them from the beam above the barrels.

"Busy night Nell", he said. "Even for a market day. Produce must have sold well in town".

Nell nodded. She crossed to the fire, and arranged the embers ready for the couvre feu .... an inverted pottery bowl that would keep the fire glowing .... alive, but safely covered, during the night hours.

"Let the fire burn for a moment Nell", said her father. "I've a mind to sit a while with you".

He brought a dark bottle, and two small cups to the curved settle by the fire. Nell smiled at him, and seated herself on a stool on the opposite side of the flames.

"Are we to share a night cap", she asked.

Her father poured a measure of brandy into each of the cups. He passed one to Nell, then sat admiring his daughter, as the flickering light from the fire played over her face and hair, over her bodice, and over her long skirts. He could so readily see her mother in the girl before him.

"We'll drink this .... and then to bed", he said. He yawned. "Early to bed, and early to rise, makes a man healthy .... and wise".

Nell laughed.

"You forgot to mention "wealthy"", she said.

Her father shook his head.

"It has never made me wealthy", he laughed, "Unless I count you as my treasure .... and I'm well content to do just that".

"The saying governs men", said Nell. "What promise can "early to bed" make to one of my sex".

"A swollen tummy", said her father .... and then a little brandy went the wrong way .... as he laughed over his own joke.

Nell went behind .... and beat him between the shoulders till he had recovered.

"And serve you right for such a jest to your own daughter", she said. ".... 'twas a joke best suited to the ale tent at a fair".

"I'm sorry Nell" he said. "As usual, you are right to correct my failings. I have run an ale house for far too many years, it seems, that my jests should make a lady blush".

They sat quietly for a moment, enjoying the peace, and this quiet time together, after the hustle and bustle of the evening. Nell looked to her father. This brandy was a rare treat. She had guessed that it would have a price ....

"What will you decide about young Giles, Nell", he asked her.

Nell looked long and hard into his eyes. He held his gaze, waiting to see what she would say.

"Giles is a young man of great virtue", she said. "He would make any girl a fine husband ....".

Her father nodded, and went to speak .... but Nell raised her hand to quiet him.

" .... but what if I were to tell him where I was last night Father. Do you know where I was bedded last night".

He shook his head.

"It is little business of mine", he said, "But I walked out for a breath of cool air some time around midnight. I saw the black mare tethered and grazing, under the shadows, by the mill".

" .... and I pray that your eyes could guide you in the moonlight, but that your ears might fail you", she said.

"Nell", he replied. "A Tavern keeper's ears are trained by long experience. They hear many things .... but needs must excercise great discretion in their meaning and import".

Nell nodded.

"You know what I have chosen for myself", she said. "Will you make strong objection .... will you persuade me from my folly".

He rose, looked to Nell, and gently covered the fire.

"No Nell", he said. "When I was at my greatest need with your mother ....".

He sighed.

"No my Nell", he said. "I'll make no objection. I'll raise no persuasion ....".

He paused ....

"But promise me this", he said, "Guard your heart, and your happiness. Those are part of the treasure I spoke of earlier. The treasure a daughter has for her father".

"I promise you father", she said. She stood and embraced him. He kissed her forehead and left the room.

Nell watched him go. She gathered her cloak and bonnet from the lobby, checked the room and the fire one final time, and went out into the night. She carried her cloak on her arm. It was a warm night, and she would have but a short walk to the mill.

THREE

Nell was startled by the brightness of the moonlight as she ran down the three steps at the front entrance of the Ship. Despite the warmth of the evening, she took her dark brown cloak and pulled it around her to conceal her white bodice and apron. In truth, it would have been wiser to leave the tavern by it's rear door, but there was no easy route from there to the mill, there being no reason, as she supposed, for the two businesses to have such convenient connection.

She turned to her left, walked a few yards, then turned to the left again, between the brick gate pillars that marked the road to the mill. Deep in the shadow there, she felt secure from prying gaze. A nightjar startled her with it's shrieking call. She paused, her momentary fright having made her suddenly aware that the path in life she now pursued had no promises of safety or security. She thought back to that morning in April, some two years previously ....

The Inn had been booked in the afternoon for a private gathering .... in fact, a funeral wake, and Nell thinking to bring some cheer and colour to the tables had, with her father's consent, gone to an area of woodland well known for it's abundance of Bluebells. She was delighted to find the area in full bloom when she arrived .... a carpet of blue in all directions. There was but a slight breeze, and with the sun growing stronger by the minute, her task in filling her basket was a pleasant one. She spied a patch of primroses, and liking the contrast in colour that they presented, she started to add their blooms to her harvest. It was then that her intuition suggested that she was not alone ....

She stood from her labours, and looked around.

Some twenty yards away, a young man sat watching her, mounted on a black horse. Nell knew enough of horses to recognise it as a fine blood mare .... the mount of a gentleman. And yet the term did not seem quite appropriate for this new arrival amongst these Bluebells. She would have suffered some consternation, aware that she was alone here, and at some distance from any habitation, but the young man showed no inclination to dismount. He removed his tricorn hat in deference, and smiled openly for her benefit.

"Good morning to you", he called. "What a pretty sight for any traveller on this sunny morn".

Nell blushed, and suspecting a compliment in his words, she decided on a parry.

"It is indeed a fine sight Sir", she said. "Have you come to gather blooms. I believe there are quite sufficient for all".

He laughed, and stretched in his seat, his great riding coat parting to reveal holstered pistols to each side of the saddle.

"No", he said. "I spied the colour from a way off and rode over to admire. And I can freely say that my trouble has been well rewarded by the pleasure now afforded to my eyes".

Again, the compliment was there, but modesty forbade that she recognise it. Nell strove to change the direction of his discourse.

"Have you ridden far this morning Sir", she asked. "I see that you have a very fine mount".

The young man nodded in appreciation of her words.

"Indeed I do", he said. "And it seems that she must have the duty of introducing us, there being no other obvious candidate for that role".

He tapped the mare on her neck. She raised her head and whinnied.

Nell laughed at her willing co-operation in the proceedings.

"I am William Marseille", he said. "Christened William .... but all who would seek me must call me Jack".

Nell smiled, and curtsied .... as her friend Mary, a lady of breeding, had taught her.

"I am Nell Mansell", she said. "My father is Tom Mansell, Landlord of the Ship Inn at Owslebury".

"Ah .... the Ship", he said. "I have heard of the house, and yet not had the pleasure of a visit to its rooms .... but I have heard that the ale to be had there is of fine reputation".

"Indeed it is Sir", Nell replied. "My father is at great pains to serve a fine beverage. Might we have the pleasure of your company in the Inn later in the day Sir".

Jack laughed.

"When I meet your father", he said, "I must tell him that he can find no fault in his daughter's recommendation of his house".

Nell stooped to gather up her basket.

"In fact", Jack added, "I have a notion to visit this Inn 'ere I grow but an hour older. May I offer you assistance in the jouney Miss Mansell".

"Nell will suffice for an Inn keeper's daughter", she said. "And I thank you for the offer Sir. However, I see that you have but one mount, and it would barely suffice for two".

"You think so", said Jack. He touched the mare foreward with his heel, and rode over to her.

"Stand still, and clutch your basket", he said.

And with a speed and dexterity so unexpected that Nell could never understand how it had been accomplished, he leaned from the saddle, and gathered her up as though she were her own rag doll, and sat her astride the mare's neck before him.

"Is that comfortable", he asked.

"Hardly comfortable Sir", she said, "When you have placed me astride your mounts neck, and the saddle sits behind me".

He laughed at her confusion.

"How far is it to the Inn", he said.

"Just a mile as we must ride Sir", she replied, shifting a little, to reposition her basket.

Jack clicked his tongue, and urged the mare to walk on.

"Just a mile then", he said. "Let us hope that in such great distance your discomfort might yet find some compensation".

He put an arm around her waist, to steady her in her seat, then to ease her burden, he took the basket of Bluebells from her grasp, and carried it in his own right hand.

He had no hands for the reins, but seemed quite content in guiding the mare with his knees.

Nell sat up straight. She could feel the pommels of his pistols against the back of her thighs. She had turned sixteen years old just a few days before. If she had been a child then, she now realised that this young man saw her as a woman. She breathed in. An aroma of leather, and horse, the black powder of his pistols, and somewhere behind these, a scent that caused her some disquiet. The scent of a stranger .... with his arm around her waist.

FOUR

The nightjar cried again, then went it's way between the trees across from the Inn. Nell stirred, some thought made her check the silver cross on it's chain around her neck. It was precious to her .... a gift from Jack. The symbol of her Faith, and yet she felt to keep it well hidden from public gaze as she knelt to her prayers in the Church on Sunday mornings, lest the Minister should enquire concerning it's history.

She turned again to the lane that led to the mill, having to exercise great care that she should not stumble in the winter ruts left by waggon wheels. The mill was currently out of use, it having broken a shaft in it's internal mechanisms. The only available mill wrights were fully employed upon the construction of a new mill some eight miles away. There was talk in the tap room that this old mill was hardly worth the expense of repair, but Nell knew that Giles had approached it's owner .... the Master of Boyes Farm ....with a view to acquiring the mill as an adjunct to his new arable farming enterprise. She also knew that Giles had examined the mill in the company of the village's Blacksmith, and it's Carpenter, and all were in agreement that repairs could be effected economically using local skills and materials. Nell had little doubt that in a year's time, the mill would once again be fully operational, with Giles as it's new master.

This lack of use, however, had left the mill lane in a parlous state .... all too likely to twist the ankle of any unwary traveller.

The lane opened out into the wider expanse of the mill yard proper .... at the moment, flooded with moonlight. The sweeps stood skeletal against the sky, the canvas of the common sails having been removed for safe keeping, pending repairs to the mill's internal workings.

Nell looked around. It took her some minutes of careful study to spot Jack's horse, secure in a loose box to the left of the yard. The animal, she knew, had been trained to exercise quietness in her behaviour when her master was not present. Nell smiled. The mare was bedded for the night: Jack felt no need to prepare for sudden departure. He would be in the brick round house built under the wooden body, or buck, of the mill.

Having learned that the mill was out of comission, Jack had been able to rent the round house, on the condition that he would vacate his possession once repairs were completed. He had made this arrangement following Giles' inspection of the mill workings, and Nell did not know if Giles knew of Jack's arrangement with John Boyes. Nor did she care to enquire. Jack was a master of discretion, his activities requiring skills in this direction, and Nell felt that Giles' heart would not grieve over what his eyes could not see.

Nell crossed the mill yard to the round house, and followed the path around to the single entrance door. Here she paused. In a few moments she would fashion her lips to tune a whistle .... the signal that she and Jack were accustomed to use, that each might know of the other's presence.

The events of the day made her want to tarry, to reflect on how she had arrived here .... arrived to stand under an abandoned mill in the moonlight, soon to announce her presence with a whistle. A signal that would lead her into the arms of her lover. A love with no promise made of marriage or security. Is this truly what she desired. She began to reflect upon her union with Jack .... and, as usual, such reflection held her in a reverie.

Used only, as she was, to the governance and care of her own soft flesh, blessed with it's plentiful curvature, she had found her first intimacies with Jack quite startling. She wondered at the hardness and muscularity of his frame, the flatness of his chest, and the natural strength of his limbs, so different from her own frailties. Her alarm at what must be her feminine part in their physical relationship, was replaced at first by seemly, if rueful acceptance .... and then ultimately by great joy, as she learned for herself, amidst some instruction from Jack, that although yes, she must, as a woman, to some degree acquiesce in their activities, she soon came to the discovery of the powers allotted her by her Maker .... power and skills in the direction of their love .... that perhaps her mother might have shared with her, had she known a mother's instruction in such matters.

As Jack lay peacefully in slumber next to her, his arm laid casually around the curve of her hips, she knew that she had been the means by which his active nature and exertions had been quelled, stilled to gentle sleep at her side. If she lay there, to grow ever more familiar with the soft chafing of her skin, the inevitable bruising of those parts of her that must take Jack's handling, however considerate he was, a bruising so tenderly administered to be sure, but magnified in her mind by her longing to keep their recent love alive in her mind .... she lay, not only happy with his care for her, but content that she had fulfilled her role in that which one alone could not do, but must needs two of like mind, if differing physicality.

Her first month with Jack had it's joy somewhat clouded by the knowledge that the day would inevitably arrive, when through want of feminine neccessity, she must turn aside his attentions. She blushed now, to remember Jack's amusement at her prudery. How, indeed, he had laughed at her concerns .... and .... to her confusion, but no little pleasure .... had stripped her of her clothing, and worshipped her body as though nothing was amiss. Such a complete intimacy was so beyond her imagination, so beyond her expectations, that she was unable to dwell on it's contemplation, but must needs simply accept it as part of her new role. The new role of a contented young woman, in a full and loving relationship.

FIVE

Nell had woken feeling thoroughly out of sorts. Her ill humour was not improved when she drew her chamber curtains, to discover that a spell of cooler weather had arrived, the view being quite spoiled by a curtain of drizzling rain falling steadily from a leaden sky. Her month had but a few days to her discomfort. She felt tense, and irritable .... a condition not improved by Jack's absence for some five days in a row. She knew well the failings of her sex, in that she must oftimes be wondering if there were other women in his life, and that he might, even now, be waking in another's bed.

She determined to resolve the issue with him upon their next encounter. She had not long to wait .... more's the pity. Had the question remained un-asked till her equilibrium had been restored, the consequences might have been less painful ....

She had gone to the mill yard that afternoon to search for an errant hen, who she suspected had gone broody, in a nest concealed from easy gaze. By chance she had arrived just as Jack was dismounting from his mare. He smiled, and walked towards her, a little puzzled that she did not run to embrace him, as was her normal custom when they had been parted.

He put his arms around her, but she remained stiff, and unyielding. Detecting her change of mood, he held her at arm's length, and looked at her quizically.

"Jack", she said. "Where have you been so many days. I fret without you, and fear that you keep company with another woman".

She regretted the words almost before they were uttered. With a speed, strength, and dexterity that, to be truthful, Nell had experience of, and therefore reason to expect, Jack threw her bodily over his bended knee, clasping her wrists firmly in the small of her back. She felt her skirts swept above her head, the cool air as her shift was pulled upwards, and the searing pain as Jack applied his riding switch to her soft bare flesh. She suffered six cutting blows in rapid pace, and such was her distress that she must have cried out for help, had not the indignities of her situation been painfully apparent to her.

Jack stood her upright again. She stared at him through angry tears, extended her finger nails, and swung a blow at him that would surely have scored his face, had he not grabbed her arm, and easily returned her to her former position with, once again, her skirts above her head. This time he satisfied himself with just four more cuts of his switch, before standing her upright once more.

"When I met you amongst the bluebells", he said, "you were little more than a child. I chose to treat you as a lady. Now you have grown to that position, you choose to act like a child, and have little cause to complain if I reward you as such for your words".

Nell stared at him.

"Go from here", she said, "and never return".

"If that is your wish", said Jack, and he turned towards his mare.

Nell rushed from the yard, and took sanctuary in her chamber. She threw herself on the bed, and cried bitterly. The physical pain was but a small component of her emotions. She had, out of her meanness of heart, tested her lover, and must now lament the consequences of her actions. She lay there for an hour, becoming ever more sure, as the minutes passed, that she could never face Jack again, even were he to pursue their acquaintanceship after such an incident.

Eventually she calmed, and discovered that the erstwhile cause of her tantrums was upon her, the physical elements of the afternoon having, no doubt, precipitated such matters. She had just set to remedy her intimate condition, when her solace was interrupted by a knock on her chamber door.

"A visitor in the parlour for you Miss Nell", said a voice. It was Anne, the kitchen maid, arrived early, to help prepare for a supper to be held that evening.

"Tell him I have no wish to endure his company", said Nell, assuming that her visitor was Jack.

There was silence from the other side of the door.

"I'm sorry, Miss Nell", said Anne. "It's a lady to see you. I believe it is Mary Long from Chalk Dell at the bottom of Whaddon Hill".

Nell's heart lept. There was no person whom she would have welcomed more at this moment. No person to whom she could narrate her distress more readily, than her dear friend Mary Long.

"Anne", she said, "Please inform Mary that I am temporarily indisposed .... but hope to quickly remedy my embarassment. I promise to join her in the parlour as soon as is manageable".

She heard Anne's steps on the wooden stairs, and set about the usual remedy of her condition. She then washed the tears from her face, combed her hair, put on a fresh white apron, and adjusted her countenance to one more suited to greet a dear friend.

SIX

Nell ran down the stairs, and through to the parlour at the rear of the Inn. It was a smaller and more comfortably furnished chamber than the common tap room, and could be accessed via a short passage to an outside door at the left of the building. In quieter moments, however, most people took the route that Nell now followed .... through the tap room.

Mary stood to greet Nell. They embraced fondly, and went to be seated, but Nell, to her great embarassment, found that she must remain standing, if her attentions to her friend were not to be distracted by acute discomfort.

Mary surveyed Anne with some obvious amusement.

"Oh my poor Nell", she said, "Are you most awfully injured".

Nell looked at her friend in bafflement.

"Then you know I have been beaten", she said.

"I do", said Mary, "and with your distress foremost in my mind, I have come as soon as I was able, to offer such comfort as might be required".

Nell stood for a second, the tears welled in her eyes, and she rushed into her friends arms. Her emotion must out, and she sobbed pitifully against Mary's shoulder.

Mary simply held Nell until this diplay of her wretchedness reached the calm that always follows such an impassioned outburst.

As the storm subsided, Mary gently prised herself from Nell's embrace. She folded her own cloak into a makeshift cushion, placed it on the chair, and bade Nell be seated upon it.

Nell sat, lowering her eyes in shame.

"Oh Nell", said Mary. "Which pains you most. Your pride, your physical discomfort .... or is it perhaps your heart".

Despite herself, and despite the throb from her injuries, she could not help but smile at her friend's intuitive perception of her present confusion.

Mary passed her a linen handkerchief, and she began to dry her eyes.

"I fear I will never see him again", she said. "Tell me it is otherwise, and I will readily bear the promise of such ministry as I was blessed with this afternoon, accepting it as my due, were I to act again as I did".

Mary laughed at her friend.

"Nell", she said, "I see that you have learned a great lesson this afternoon. That even the most wonderful things can be spoiled if they are treated carelessly. Indeed the more wonderful they are, the more care needest be taken in their maintenance. And when the maintenance concerns the relationship between two living bodies, and their inhabiting souls, then that maintenance is a skill that takes much time and application to master".

"I have most certainly been mastered this afternoon", said Nell.

"That was not my meaning", said Mary. "Jack is well able to master you in the way you have now experienced, but if we are to consider pain of the heart, then you have surely mastered Jack, because as I look at you now, I can assure you of no lesser a pain in Jack's heart than in your own".

"How can this be", said Nell. "It was I who was punished so cruelly".

"Did you not intend to punish Jack when you rose this morning. Did you not plan to confront him with an accusation for which you had not the slightest evidence or reason".

Nell blushed, barely able to allow Mary a view of her countenance.

"I'm sorry", she said.

"Ah", said Mary, "and in those two words lie the secret of relationship. You say them readily to me. Can you look at Jack, with your heart bared to his gaze, and utter those two words so readily".

"Were I granted the opportunity, I believe in my heart that I could", said Nell.

Mary stood, preparing to take her leave.

"Then let us hope that such opportunity is not long withheld from you", she said.

Nell rose also, retrieving the cloak on which she sat, and returning it to her friend.

"And in the meantime", said Mary, "you have some little pain to sharpen your mind, and to keep you true to your resolve".

Nell took her friend's wrist, as though to restrain her.

"How did you know", she asked.

Mary took her hand and pressed it between her own.

"Jack knew of our friendship", she said. "He came to ask for my help in your management. And although it is true that you and I are friends of long standing , I could not easily have declined his plea, such was his sorrow at your condemnation of him".

Nell fell silent. She saw Mary to the entrance, and there kissed her farewell. She returned thoughtfully to her chamber, to lay undisturbed whilst she considered, most carefully, the content of their discussion.

SEVEN

It came as little surprise, some two days later, when Anne approached Nell in the tap room with a letter.

"Begging your pardon Miss", she said, "but a boy just arrived with this letter for you from Mary Long".

Nell took the folded sheet, and broke the wax seal that held the document closed.

"Are you quite well Miss", asked Anne. "We couldn't help but notice you seem different in yourself these last two days"

Nell smiled at her concern.

"I am quite well thank you Anne", she said. I suffered an accident that caused me some bruising, but it is only superficial, and I will be quite mended in a day or two".

Anne looked as though she were about to make further enquiry, but a call from Nell's father sent her hurrying back to the kitchen .... to Nell's considerable relief .... as further information, regarding the cause of her discomfort, was not something she cared to impart.

She looked at the sheet in her hand, and was delighted to find an invitation to supper at Chalk Dell cottage from her friend Mary Long. The invitation was for the following Monday, an evening that Mary would realise would be quiet in the Inn, thereby making it possible for Nell to be spared from her normal duties.

Nell went immediately to her chamber for pen and paper, and wrote an acceptance. She folded the sheet, sealed it, as was customary, with a wax stick held in a candle flame, and took it, with three penny pieces, to Anne who would arrange for it's delivery to Chalk Dell Cottage. Nell had not asked her father's permission for the excursion, but she felt sure that he would raise no objection .... especially because her father believed that his daughter was want to follow her friend's advice, and he had often expressed a hope that Mary might dissuade Nell from the path she had apparently chosen.

By the Saturday morning before her keenly anticipated invitation, Nell was all but recovered. Truth to tell, her flesh still showed some evidence of Jack's ministry, but the marks were now all but faded. Nell had examined these colourful proofs of her adventures, in a glass, remembering as she did so, Jack's words following their application: That she had acted like a child, and could not therefore complain if she was treated as such for her misdemeanours. The bruising may have faded .... but his words still stung her cruelly. She was not yet so old, that to be referred to as a child, could not bring tears of frustration to her eyes.

It was unusual .... very unusual .... for Jack to return to the mill on a Saturday. Friday and Saturday were important days for those in his profession, so it was with great surprise that Nell found Bess stabled in the usual loose box when she went to check on the broody hen. Her first thought was to flee to her chamber, but remembering Mary's admonitions, she composed herself, and continued towards the mill. It was some comfort, as she continued, slowly but resolutely, that she had bathed herself, and donned fresh clothes earlier in the day.

"Good afternoon Nell".

It was Jack. He was seated on the wooden flight of steps that ascended to the mill body. He was wearing a blue riding coat that Nell had not seen before. His hair was trimmed, and he was freshly shaven. If absence makes the heart grow fonder, she could hardly have loved him more than she did at that moment. He sat there in the sun, with his account book on his knee, and smiled at her, as though nothing had happened between them.

Nell immediately walked across the yard, and stood before him with her eyes downcast. He came down from his perch and stood looking at her.

"I am truly sorry for my behaviour Jack", she whispered. "Can you find it in your heart to forgive me".

"Oh Nell", he said. "I forgave you even as you sped away from me".

She rushed into his arms. He wrapped them around her, and she, in her turn, held him tighter than perhaps ever before.

"Are you still in pain from your treatment", he asked her.

Nell laughed happily.

"No Jack", she said, "but your words concerning the behaviour of children .... and their appropriate treatment .... still cause my face to burn with embarassment".

He raised her face to his, and kissed her full on the mouth.

"Does that medicine ease your affliction", he asked.

"Kind Sir, a little more of this medicine, if you can spare it", sighed Nell.

Jack indeed had medicine to spare. They stood in the sun, by the mill, and Jack proved himself the equal of any physician in alleviating her ills.

By neccessity, Nell must return to her evening duties in the tap room, but Jack had come in for the final hour, and had sat playing cribbage with John Boyes .... the owner of the mill.

Although Nell glanced admiringly at him many times .... by tacit agreement they never displayed any sign of their mutual affection when customers were present in the Inn. Had there been members of her own sex present, Nell doubted that their arrangement would have fooled any with the slightest powers of observation. The normal clientele, however, were mainly farm workers and tradesmen .... all of whom were male .... and therefore unlikely, as Nell well knew, to spot a romantic affiliation unless they were treated to a public display of she and Jack kissing in full embrace. And even then she was far from certain of the result.

She slept with Jack that night. Their love making had been unhurried, and exceptionally gentle. Perhaps Jack felt the need to woo her affections, as if from the very start of their relationship. As they lay in the candlelight, Nell told of her invitation for the following Monday evening. Jack expressed approval and said he was sure she would enjoy her supper with Mary.

Nell broached the subject of her chastisement at Jack's hands just one more time. She felt the need to impart that which she had shared with Mary, namely that during her solace in her chamber, before her friend's visit, she had realised that she would readily accept the risk of future correction by Jack, of the nature she had experienced, if Jack were willing to take her in his arms once again, and profess that he loved her.

Nell had shared this with Mary .... and with Jack .... supposedly to indicate that her lesson had indeed been taken to heart, and that she would never, in the future, act to precipitate such reaction from her lover.

But deep within her, Nell knew that she was terribly prone to the effects of the monthly ebb and flow of her emotions, and she admitted to herself, in private, that she could offer no guarantees of such virtue as she had professed.

And deeply buried beneath her covers, in her private chambers, above the entrance to the Inn, she must face, with mortification, that should she be the cause of a future incident, then she would lay across Jack's knee obediently, with no hint of protest, to receive joyfully such gifts as he might bestow upon her.

Because, again, if she were to truly bare her sole .... and by neccessity, must bare it with her cheeks aflame .... she would confess that her mastery by Jack that afternoon had provided her with the most exciting and pleasurable moments of her young life .... not withstanding the discomforts that it had afforded her.

EIGHT

The day for her excursion to Chalk Dell had dawned bright and fair, but to Nell's consternation, the afternoon had turned cloudy, and she wondered if she could possibly arrive at her friend's residence without a wetting.

As Nell had expected, her father raised no objection to the visit. He privately approved of the friendship, and did all he could to encourage it. Mary Long, as he knew, was a lady of breeding, albeit one of a most extraordinary history.

Nell set out at six pm expecting to arrive comfortably for the time Mary had proposed in her invitation.

She carried a bouquet of flowers, admittedly gathered from the hedgerows (but none the less attractive for that), and a small bottle of Jerez wine .... a gift to Mary from her father.

Nell was fortunate in that she arrived at the cottage door just as the first drops of rain began to fall. She was shown into the parlour by Gwen, Mary's housemaid, a cheerful and intelligent girl from the village, that Mary had taken under her wing. She had offered Gwen's parents some education for their daughter in reading, writing, simple mathematics, and music, in exchange for domestic assistance.

Mary stood to greet her visitor.

"Thank you for coming at such short notice", she said .... embracing Nell, and placing a kiss on her forehead.

"It was a great pleasure to receive your invitation", said Nell, "and once again I must thank you for your timely visit in the hour of my distress".

"I was relieved to receive you in the inn parlour", said Mary, "even though you appeared somewhat reluctant to be seated".

Nell winced at the memory. She proffered her gifts. The flowers were much admired, and Gwen was summoned to bring drinking cups for the Jerez wine.

"So thoughtful of your father", said Mary. "We shall eat our supper in my small dining room, and against the chill of this unseasonal evening, I have asked Gwen to lay a fire for our comfort."

Gwen returned with a tray bearing two small cups and the bottle of Jerez.

"Is the fire in the dining room now alight Gwen", Mary asked her.

"It is indeed Miss Mary", said Gwen, "But it might be that you would wish to tarry here while the room warms".

"Thank you for your thoughtfulness Gwen. You are a great boon to me", said Mary.

She motioned Nell to be seated.

"I apologise for the chill", she said but this most unexpected change in the weather has caught us unprepared. We shall soon, I hope, be able to adjourn to the dining room".

The two women sat. Nell glanced around the room. For a humble country cottage it was very well decorated and furnished, a fact that gave hint to her friend's most unusual domestic arrangements.

Mary passed Nell her cup of wine from the tray that Gwen had left on a small side table. They each took an inital sip.

"Again", said Mary, "you must thank your father for me. This is a much appreciated treat".

"I'm sure he bestowed it very gladly", said Nell.

"And so", said Mary, "Are you now fully recovered from your recent distress".

Nell laughed.

"I am quite recovered, thank you", she said.

Mary looked at her thoughtfully.

"And perhaps you now view your discomfort in a more favourable light", she said.

Nell coloured. This apparent ability of her friend, Mary, to view her innermost soul, could be very alarming.

Mary laughed.

"Oh my Nell", she said, "Our maker chose to install the most complex of emotions into the original design of his fairest creation. Let us be thankful that he did not equally bestow such complexity upon his original model, or imagine what we women must endure from our male companions upon this Earth".

Nell laughed as she perceived her friends meaning, and did her best to recover her composure, having had what she truly believed to be her most carefully concealed feelings, apparently so readily examined.

There was a tap at the parlour door.

"If it please you Miss", said Gwen, "The supper is prepared, and the room now warm enough for your comfort".

Nell, at her friend's request took up the tray with it's bottle and vessels, and followed Mary through to the dining room. Gwen saw them carefully seated, before withdrawing to make final arrangements for the meal to be served.

The supper was a great success. There was a roast partridge for each of them, a variety of cottage garden vegetables, and to Nell's interest and delight, a steaming bowl of potatoes, a delicacy which she herself had not seen before. She had expected a strong flavour .... but following Mary's direction in the application of both butter, and a little salt, found this novelty most palatable.

Mary herself had made what she knew to be a favourite dessert for Nell. "Bread and butter" pudding. A confection of bread, fruits, and custard, baked in the oven until the crust was a golden brown.

Mary requested a freshly made pot of tea be brought .... another treat for Nell .... but they decided to allow Gwen to clear the table, and, carrying their tea, returned to the parlour, pleased to discover that the thoughtful maid, needing no guidance from her mistress, had kindled a fire against their return.

They sat comfortably in front of the hearth, Mary placing the tea kettle upon a brass trivet near the flames.

"I must confess that I had a purpose in inviting you to supper this evening", she said.

Gwen had suspected as much, but waited for Mary to collect her thoughts and share her intent.

"Your father is much concerned for your welfare", Mary said. "He has spoken with me upon the subject".

This was little surprise to Nell. Indeed .... there were times when she must need examine her own actions in relation to her future well being.

"Giles Barnes is a handsome young man with excellent prospects", said Mary. "His hard working nature and industry in diverse projects of commerce are much admired. There are many young ladies in this area who view him as a very desirable future husband".

Nell coloured.

"Giles has all but made a proposal to me", she said. "I have only to offer the slightest encouragement ....".

She paused .... uncertain as to how she might continue.

"But you will not have him", asked Mary.

"How can I have him when every vessel of my heart overflows with thoughts for Jack", said Nell. "You, of all my friends must see that".

Mary took up the tea kettle, and refreshed their cups.

"You are correct", she said. "I of all people .... but please do not be mistaken. You do not disappoint me in your reply my dearest Nell. In truth I must have thought the less of you had you responded in another manner".

"My dearest friend", said Nell. "I have some small knowledge of your history. Will you not share all, in the hope that it might assist me in my confusion".

"If you believe it will help", said Mary. "I will confess it would be something of a relief to share with you .... and it may prove to be a pleasant enough distraction for us both on this wet evening".

Mary summoned Gwen and asked for a fresh pot of tea. It having been brought, she bade Gwen retire for the night, explaining that they intended to sit on, but were happy to provide for themselves such small additions as might be required for their immediate comfort.

Gwen wished them both a good night, and retired.

"Where to begin", said Mary, smiling at Nell.

"At the beginning", suggested Nell .... and they both laughed.

NINE

"I am the eldest daughter of the great house of Marwell Hall", said Mary.
"I was born there, under it's roof, and Christened there, in the private chapel. Mary Alice Long is the name upon my certificate of Baptism".

"And yet you choose to dwell in a humble cottage", said Nell.

Mary smiled.

" .... and yet I choose to dwell in a humble cottage", she agreed. She looked to the door.

"We have some time yet before John returns", she said. She rose from her chair and went to a small bureau in the corner. She was occupied for a moment, then finding the document she sought, she passed it to Nell.

"It is my certificate of Marriage to John", she said, "Issued in London, far from the eyes of local people".

Nell perused the paper.

"This must have taken great courage and fortitude on both your parts", she said.

"Yes", said Mary, "Perhaps most would say the greater courage from myself .... but that is not neccessarily true .... that matter of the nature of male emotions we talked of earlier has it's bearing here".

Nell nodded

"Tell me the story", she asked.

Mary returned to her seat, and sat staring into the fire. She added another log to the flames.

"The Hall entered an era of great prosperity, as I grew up there", she said. "And in this we must grant my father his full due. He was by all accounts, and still is, a shrewd business man. As well as the estate itself he had diverse interests in many centres of our population. He soon grew wealthy enough to be able to indulge his dream of extending the Hall with more modern, and comfortable apartments. A london architect accepted the commission, and the southern-most area of our home soon became the site of intense activity".

"And you showed an interest in these improvements", asked Nell.

"I did indeed", said Mary. "I took upon myself the social welfare of the craftsmen, and their families, who came to live on the estate for the duration of the works. This, you understand, was a project expected to provide them with employment for several years, and therefore the craftsmen, the labourers, all had to be accommodated that the work could proceed uninterupted by the delay and difficulties of travel for those involved. Several out-houses were hastily converted for accommodation, and several nearby disused cottages recommissioned for the arriving families".

"Did your father approve of your social concerns", asked Nell

"He was bemused by them", said Mary. "His concern was for the works themselves, and he seemed to have given little thought to the lives of those who would turn his project into reality. But once I had explained to him, that by the least artifice, and some small kindnesses, of little if any expense, the labourers could be kept happy in their endeavours, he cautiously allotted me a small budget, and bade me do the best I could to maintain a productive atmosphere at the works, and a helpful and conducive domestic peace, in the homes of those who had joined us".

"Is that how you met John", said Nell.

"It is", said Mary. "He was Foreman to the bricklayers on the site, a master of his craft, and with six young men under his instruction. And woe betide them if their work did not meet his exacting standards. He was always on site before his men, always last to leave, and had the personal responsibility of the most complex areas of brick work in the design, the execution of which neccessitated that he and my father's architect were in frequent consultation".

She paused for thought.

"It was a happy time for me", she said. "I would rise, eat a hasty breakfast, then go about my rounds of visiting the worker's families. There were several young mothers, with children. I would sit with them, and if their domestic situation left them wanting, I would do my best to provide a solution. Perhaps a crib for a new baby .... there were three born during the works .... perhaps simply to sit with small children whilst the mother suffered some indisposition. I did what I could, and my efforts in this direction seemed much appreciated. I soon extended my rounds to include the estate workers cottages .... fearing that they might otherwise envy the care bestowed upon the new arrivals".

"Did your father approve of that", said Nell in surprise.

"He most definitely did not", said Mary, "But I persisted in my arguments, and it was soon apparent, even to him, that the harmony and productivity of the estate were so much improved, that he wondered he had not set such simple welfare arrangements in place of his own initiative".

Nell laughed in delight.

"I had heard that the Marwell estate has an extraordinary ability to retain it's staff", she said, "And you, my dear Mary, were the cause".

Mary smiled ruefully.

"Do not think that it always went so smoothly", she said. "The most avid of social carers must tread with great caution when the relationship between a young husband and his wife is concerned".

Nell blushed at these words. They would have meant nothing to her a short while ago but now ....

"It was in such a situation of unrest that I was first thrown into society with John", she said. "He sought me out with concerns over a newly arrived couple. The young fellow concerned was a carpenter .... not immediately under John's supervision .... but a problem of design had apparently arisen where only the close co-operation of the bricklayers, and the carpenters, could resolve the difficulties".

"And John had spotted a domestic unrest", asked Nell.

"He had", said Mary. "The young fellow concerned seemed arrogant from the start. His wife had given birth to twin boys, and he was unpleasantly boastful of his prowess in fathering these sons. When John declared his intention of visiting, that he might pay his respects to the mother, and admire these fine infants , the young man made excuse, and it was not long before John heard that the young mother was curiously reluctant to socialise with the other wives, indeed she had never been seen outside of her cottage".

"John asked you to investigate", said Nell, leaning forwards, in her interest to hear the outcome of this narrative.

"I would have soon visited in any event", said Mary, "but a bad head cold had limited my activities for several days. However, having heard John's concerns, it was my very first port of call on the following morning".

"What did you find", asked Nell.

"What John suspected", said Mary. "The cottage was well kept, and scrupulously clean. The infants bonny and very well cared for. I had no concerns for their welfare. But the mother stayed in the shadows during my visit, and it was only upon my insistence that her well being was my utmost concern, that she stepped forward for me to better view her condition".

"Oh dear", said Nell, "I believe I might guess ....".

"You might", said Mary. "She was a pretty girl, with a petite figure, and with a fine head of dark curls. She swept her curls aside to show the bruising on her face. There was a cut healing on her forehead, and she broke down and cried pitifully when I asked that she remove her bodice. Reluctantly she complied. Her torso was covered in bruising. I was horrified. I sought the assistance of a nearby family, a mother, and her oldest daughter. We gathered up the infants, and such things as were immediately required for their care, and I shepherded her back to the hall, and established her in my own apartments, pending a decision about her future. She cried with relief that she had been rescued from the cruelty of her husband. Having calmed her emotions, I directed her to the care of her children, trusting that such labour would provide her with happy distraction, whilst I sought remedy for her situation".

Later that evening, when work was over for the day, I visited John, and layed the unhappy situation before him. He was as horrified as I . We did however have one thing to assist us. The young woman had confessed to me, in her distress, that she and this young carpenter, were not formally married. In fact he had applied for his position at these works to escape his home village, bringing the girl and her babes with him .... in her case to escape the admonition of her parents".

"They were really not married", asked Nell.

"No", said Mary, "and it was of great assistance to both John and I that they were not. Asking if I were able to temporarily care and provide for the mother and her chidren, John went off to interview the young man. That interview went most unsatisfactorily, and the young carpenter was summarily dismissed, and escorted from the estate, with promises of severe consequences were he to return".

"Did he", asked Nell.

"He did not", said Mary.

"And what happened to the young mother", asked Nell.

"Matters were arranged most satisfactorily", said Mary. "Her age made her still officially a child in the law's eyes. John adopted her, and took her and her babes into his own cottage. As a master craftsman his income was sufficient to allow him to provide for her. She was a pretty girl, and it was not long before other young men on the estate sought her favours. She was properly married to a stonemason's son just eighteen months later. The couple remained here until the improvements to the hall were completed. They then returned to Oxford. They were well matched, and I believe them to be still happily married. They had two daughters together. The first born here, the second in Oxford. The boys seem likely to follow their new father into his craft.

"But you and John ....". asked Nell.

"We soon found that we enjoyed each other's company", said Mary. "He was fascinated by my concept of social care for the estate staff, and I, in turn, was interested in his craft. I would visit the works and watch him practising his skills. He taught me to understand the different brick bonds, and their applications, and I came to understand the engineering involved in building works. He was able to read, and write, had some scientific and mathematical knowledge, and even some awareness of politics. About a month before his contract at the Hall ended, I asked him to marry me".

Nell's jaw fell open in astonishment.

"You asked John", she said.

"I did", said Mary. "I persuaded my father to grant me sufficient funds to purchase these cottages. They had fallen derelict. John renovated them. He took the Southern cottage, I the North, and as far as the world at large is concerned, our relationship is the normal condition of neighbours. Here I am a bricklayers neighbour named Mary Long. I maintain my position of daughter of the house at Marwell Hall under the name Alice Long. Few know that Mary .... and Alice are one and the same. It amuses me to think that some day in the future an inquisitive historian will wonder upon the fact that Alice Long of Marwell Hall, and Mary Long of Chalk Dell Cottage died on the same day, in the same year, and in the same village. Personal histories can be a great puzzle Nell. They really can.

TEN

Mary's story had kept Nell spellbound. She found herself in need of the privy, and was directed to those offices by her hostess. The rain had ceased, and the air was refreshingly cool upon her cheeks, as she traversed the length of the garden path.

Her visit concluded, she stood surveying the cottage's horticultural arrangements, in as much as she could admire their design in the moonlight. Mary's narration had suggested certain possibilities to her young and active mind. She had known some of her friend's private history, but was still puzzled as to how she managed to maintain two remarkable, and separate lives: that of the daughter of a great house .... and that of a humble cottager. The foremost, with all the duties that Mary had described in her social cares of the estate, and the latter as a wife and mother. For Mary had two children by her husband, John Froud.

She returned to the parlour where Mary delighted her with a cup of hot chocolate. A very rare treat in a rural village such as Owslebury. The two women sat with their cups, blowing away the steam, till it should be cool enough to drink.

"Where are Mathew and Sarah tonight", asked Nell.

Mary smiled at the mention of her children.

"As I was planning this supper", she said, "there was a most happy coincidence in that John asked if I would object to his taking part in a darts tournament at the Brushmaker's Arms at Upham. I suggested that he might give the children an outing, and that he should book a room for the night in the Inn. They could travel over together at their leisure, enjoy the festivities, and return in the morning after a peaceful night's sleep, having only to traverse the stairs to their chamber when they were ready for their beds. I can assure you that there was great excitement when the children were made privy to the plan".

"And will they stay up so late", asked Nell, rather horrified at this novel exercise in the management of infants.

Mary shook her head.

"John will see them to their beds at seven", she said. ".... and the daughter of that house has promised to look in upon them whilst John is at his sport".

Nell shook her head. She could not imagine such excitement in her own childhood.

There was a pause as the two friends enjoyed their chocolate. The fire burned well in the grate, and Mary had soon to add more fuel.

"You have questions for me Nell", she said.

"I do", said Nell. "It is a great wonder to me that you can manage two lives so distinctly different in their very nature. How is that possible".

"I think I see your direction", said Mary. "But it is not so very difficult when all those involved have become familiar with the practical neccessities of it's management. It is not so very different to any craftsman, or indeed labourer, who maintains his home life, but needs must travel each and every day to his place of employment".

Nell, who had sat listening attentively, smiled at her friend's simile.

"And you find great happiness in your arrangements", she asked.

"Indeed I do", smiled Mary. "My Husband John means the world to me, and the Lord has seen fit to bless me with two fine children. John is all that they could desire in a father .... and he is, in every way, all that I could desire in a husband".

"And yet you must, by force of your position as the daughter of a great house, have been petitioned by many wealthy suitors", said Nell.

"Did they petition for my wealth and position, with a view to their own ambitions .... or did they petition for my heart", asked Mary.

"And what of your own father", asked Nell. "Did he not threaten to disown you when he learned of your plans".

"My father could indeed have disowned me", smiled Mary. "But such is the productivity and harmony of his estate, that when he compares like for like with his neighbours, he cannot help but recognise my abilities in it's social management .... and the resulting profit to his purse. My father's love of business holds sway over his emotions when he looks to my affairs".

"You show good example that a young woman should follow the guidance of her heart", said Nell.

"And I perceive that you are want to follow that same sentiment", said Mary.

Her tone in this had been that of a question.

Nell blushed.

"At least in my position", she said, "I have not the fear of the condemnation of my family and friends. I am an Inn keeper's daughter, with no great social prospects before me".

"But the role of a prosperous Yeoman farmer's wife is one of no little honour", said Mary.

Again Nell blushed that her friend should see her innermost mind so readily.

"Is that then the role you believe I should accept", she asked.

Mary stood and beckoned her friend into an embrace. They stood in the firelight tightly held in each other's arms.

"My dearest Nell", she said. "Let me ask you this. Were you to learn on the morrow that Giles had suffered such fatal calamity as beset his dear father, would then your heart grieve to the same degree as if you discovered only hours later that Jack had encountered some similar disaster".

Nell freed herself from her friend's grasp in horror. Mary studied her countenance with keen interest.

"I see we have the answer", said Mary, "And it seems that I have this evening played hostess to a young woman quite as strong in unconventionality as myself".

Nell bowed her head in shame.

"You are the daughter of a great house", she said. "How can I expect your favour, when I know full well the title I have chosen for myself".

"And what title is that", asked Mary.

"A Highwayman's Doxy", said Nell defiantly.

"And my dear Nell", said Mary. "I should not have wished for better company".

ELEVEN

It became obvious to the two friends, as they paused in their conversation, that the rain had returned with a vengeance.

"I cannot allow you to return home in such conditions", said Mary. "You must share my chamber tonight. There is a small bed set there, should one of the children need watching over. It will take but a few moments to furnish it with fresh linen".

"Could I not share with you as John is away", asked Nell.

"If that would suit you", laughed Mary. "And I could not wish for a better bedfellow in my dear husband's absence".

Having made the fire safe for the night, and extinguished all but the candles that they would need in the short journey to the bedchamber, Nell followed Mary from the parlour, and having ascended the stairs, was shown into a surprisingly spacious room, pleasantly decorated for the purposes of inducing peaceful repose.

"I must lend you a night gown", said Mary. "Fortunately Gwen assisted me in an overhaul of our linen only recently, and I can promise that all is freshly laundered and pressed. She produced a very servicable gown, and held it up for Nell's inspection.

"I'm afraid it not of the latest style", she said, smiling, "But as none other than I is likely to view it, it will suit your purpose for this one occasion".

With some neccessary, and gratefully received, mutual assistance in the management of hooks, eyes, and buttons, concerned with the fastening of their bodices, the two friends made their preparations for the night. At Mary's bequest they both knelt to pray, each privately petitioning their Creator, until Mary uttered an "Amen" that Nell accepted as the conclusion of the session.

As she pulled aside the coverlets, Mary paused.

"Would it help your repose my dear Nell", she said, "if I were to inform you that I have the germ of an idea by which your future might successfully be managed .... such as to satisfy your lust for adventure, but equally having consideration to your future peace and security".

"I cannot see that such is possible", replied Nell, "But if it were, I would indeed be delighted to hear any proposal you might make, knowing as I did, that it would be based on wisdom and experience".

Mary laughed.

"As to wisdom", she said, "Only time may tell. But experience .... perhaps yes .... my thoughts must be influenced by such experience as I have in these matters. Let me rest upon it dear Nell, in the hopes that the light of a new day might assist in the germination of the seed within my mind".

....

Mary and Nell rose with the light the next morning. The day had dawned bright and clear, and Mary's first action upon rising was to dispatch Gwen to the Ship Inn to assure Nell's father of his daughter's well being. The friends then washed and dressed, and went down to the parlour, much surprised to find Gwen quickly returned.

"If it please you Miss", said Gwen, "I had only to go half way before I encountered Anne from the Tavern sent upon a similar errand to my own. I was able to assure her of Miss Nell's safety, and she returned to impart her news. Seeing no need to duplicate it, I returned to prepare your breakfast".

Mary smiled at her.

"All is well then Gwen", said Mary. "Nell's father will be reassured".

To Nell's delight Mary requested that Gwen serve their simple breakfast at a table set outside, on a small brick paved area behind the cottage. From here they were able to enjoy a view over Mary's well kept garden.

It was a delightful morning, birdsong and scented breezes from Mary's culivated blooms adding to the pleasure of the meal.

"Have you had further thoughts concerning your final proclamation 'ere we laid our heads to rest", asked Nell.

"I have", said Mary. "I shall call Gwen that she might bring a fresh pot of coffee".

The coffee having been served, Mary collected her thoughts.

"You may think to raise objection as I suggest this plan to you Nell", she said, "but please hear me out before you add your own views .... and then, as you see fit".

Nell nodded an agreement, and took up her coffee, waiting patiently to hear her friend's proposals.

"Giles Barnes will soon have need of a manager for the domestic, and close affairs of his farm". said Mary. "He can scarce be expected to properly oversee the accounts, the dairy, the poultry, the kitchen garden, the management of the household staff, and his own sustenance, whilst he has herds to maintain, arable ventures to pursue, and visits to town and market for business matters, let alone his new plan to lease and recommission the old mill".

Nell looked puzzled.

"What then are you proposing", she asked.

Mary smiled at her.

"That you should take up paid employment with Giles in the management of those matters I have raised. With the possible exception of the dairy, you have some experience in all the things I mention, and to that last, I am sure the head dairy maid will need little supervision beyond that required to see her products put to efficient purpose".

Nell shook her head.

"But I am needed at the Tavern", she said. "Could my father so easily spare me that you suggest such a drastic change in my affairs".

"I think your father will spare you", laughed Mary, "Particularly when he sees that the plan appears to move you in a direction of which he has long held hopes".

Nell stared at her friend with astonishment.

"But how might such an affair be instigated", she said.

"You must go to Giles and set the proposal before him", said Mary.

Nell gasped as she perceived the artifice in her friend's ideas.

"And Giles will agree to this because he will also imagine that affairs appear to move in a direction he might desire, with the thoughts that it may lead to our closer union".

Mary laughed.

"And who knows what the future may hold in that respect", she said. "But your new conditions will suit your father, they will suit Giles, and they will suit you very well when you consider that you needs must make frequent visits to your old home".

"And what of Jack", said Nell. "What will he say".

Mary laughed again.

"I forsee no strong objection from your Jack", she replied. " You simply swap one employment for another, and with the little knowledge I have of men's minds, I believe your new position will be viewed with much favour by Jack, in that it places you less in the gaze of other young men who might seek your favours".

"He need have no fears in that respect", said Nell.

"So I perceive", said Mary, "but the thought will have crossed his mind .... and it can do no harm to our plans".

Nell sat shaking her head in wonder.

"And this is your advice", she said.

"It is", said Mary, "and with careful consideration you will discover that the plan has much to commend it".

TWELVE

All too aware that her absence from the Inn would be causing others no little inconvenience, Nell bade her hostess fond farewell, and made haste to return to her duties. As she strode up the hill that led to the village, her mind was active in consideration of all that had transpired during her visit to her friend.

The Inn was in some turmoil, the heavy rain of the previous evening having found it's way somehow into the cellar. The flooding, however was little more than an inconvenince, there being no damage to the stored supplies. Nell assisted in the efforts to remove the unwanted confluence, mops and buckets being the only means at their disposal. She and her father were much relieved when they were finally able to sit together for their light midday meal, with conditions below fully restored.

For the purpose of experimentation, Nell decided to enlighten her father with respect to her plans, but preferred to keep her friend Mary's role in their suggestion secret for the present.

Her father listened carefully to what she had to say. It was with some amusement that Nell observed his reaction. His initial alarm at the proposal seemed to cause him uncertainty as to how to proceed. He fell silent. Then Nell, as Mary had predicted, was able to observe the moment when he realised that this plan led his daughter in a direction that had a chance of leading to further developements. Developements of which he would heartily approve.

He drew breath.

"And is this plan of Gile's suggestion", he asked. "I would have thought that he might have spoken with me in advance of approaching my daughter".

"No, no Father. Please do not think ill of Giles", Nell replied. "Further to his visit some days ago I have been much worried by his present condition, and thought to make the proposal to him .... with your blessing, of course".

"Do you think that you could manage all that would be needed of you in the home affairs of the farm", he asked her.

"I feel I could", she said, "And at the least I must surely, by application to those home affairs, lift many small cares from Giles' shoulders".

"Then you have my blessing", he said. "As to our affairs here .... I can promote Anne to your role. She is now of an age to make that possible, and there are several young girls in the village, friends of Anne herself, who may be willing to step into her shoes, reassured by her presence as their mistress".

Nell smiled.

"Then you have no objection".

"None", he said. "But you have not yet made the proposal to Giles .... although, upon reflection, I see with some amusement that he is highly unlikely to refuse what you suggest to him".

"Then I will proceed", said Nell. She kissed her father on the forehead, and went in search of Anne, fully confident that she could warn that young lady of her coming promotion, without the fear of subsequently disappointing her.

....

Long after dark had fallen over the mill, Nell lay in Jack's arms. That he worshipped her totally and absolutely had never been more apparent than in his display of affection, both spiritual and physical, since she had joined him that night in the privacy of his makeshift abode at the mill.

She waited till he was satisfied in body and mind, and peacefully settled, before raising the subject that had been foremost in her thoughts since her interview with her friend Mary.

Jack listened without interruption.

As with her father, Nell saw initial concern change to thoughtful agreement, as the advantages of the arrangement occured to him.

"And this is your idea", he asked. "You have not been approached by Giles".

"I have not", she said, "But his predicaments are obvious to all but the most casual observer of his affairs. We have long been acquaintances, his charitable nature is well known in the village, and I would feel it a slight upon my character if I were not to offer him this help in the hour of his need".

"And you do not think to compromise your virtue", said Jack.

Nell feigned to strike him .... in jest .... but held the blow, and kissed him on his lips.

"Kind Sir", she said. "My virtue is compromised already .... as well you know .... even if your ministrations in the last hour had not proved the case beyond any reasonable doubt".

Jack laughed.

"That was not quite my meaning", he said. "Do you not think that the village will begin to prattle about the relationship between you and your new employer".

"Such prattle will be short lived", she said. "The farm is a busy one, with various staff domiciled in the house. Secret liason would be impossible, and any show of affection impossible to conceal. The relationship will be purely of a professional nature, as all will testify".

Jack smiled.

"It seems", he said, "that you have considered all aspects very thoroughly. If it was my blessing and approval that you sought, then you have both".

He smiled at her.

"But I see no reason why you should not use any means at your immediate disposal to show your gratitude", he said. "What gifts will you offer to express your thanks for such understanding and co-operation as I have shown you".

"But Kind Sir, what means can you refer to", she said, smiling at him. "For I am as lacking in means as the moment I was born. You may search my person if you wish".

"I shall indeed search", said Jack, "And I believe that contrary to this assessment of your condition, I may, with diligent application, find treasure enough to suit me very well, my sweet Nell".

She sighed and layed back upon the pillows.

"If you must", she said. "I am sure I would not know how to direct you".

....

With both Jack, and her father, now privy to her objectives, Nell looked to traverse her next hurdle. How best to approach Giles with her proposals for his assistance and welfare.

If it sometimes seems that man's actions are directed from above, this was indeed a case to prove the point. Scarce had the Inn opened on the following morning, when to Nell's astonishment, a boy arrived bearing a message from Giles himself. The boy had apparently been instructed to wait for a reply, and hearing this, Nell tore open the paper and read it's content. Finding that she needs must respond immediately, she hastened to her chamber, where she kept pen and paper, having bidden Anne to serve the young man half a pint of cool ale whilst he waited.

The communication from Giles contained an invitation to the farm, for a late breakfast, on the following morning. Giles intimated that he wished to discuss with Nell certain affairs of business, believing that his proposals might be to her personal interest and benefit.

Inevitably, Nell could not help but wonder if she and Giles were of the same mind, but this would be so fortuitous, that she could scarce set her hopes against such a conclusion. Could it be possible, she thought, that Mary had talked to Giles ....

She soon dismissed the idea however. She could not believe that Mary would ever attempt to involve herself in the practical instigation of a plan which had simply been intended as little more than one possible solution to Nell's problems. Mary had made a suggestion .... of a way forwards, should Nell decide to attempt a change in her personal situation. But Mary had clearly left the means by which the suggestion might be acted upon to Nell herself.

The invitation from Giles must therefore be considered as the result of his initiative .... and his alone. Nell looked forward, with keen anticipation, to hear of those matters that might be "to her personal interest and benefit".

FOURTEEN

There was little doubt that the weather had cooled to some degree since the heavy rains of two days ago. With a three mile walk to the farm at Morestead, Nell surveyed the skies with some concern. Her father joined her on the steps of the Inn.

"I am confident that it will stay dry for your journey", he told her. "There was a reddening of the sky in the west yesterday evening, and this greyness will have cleared in an hour, I'm sure".

Nell remained un-convinced, and hastened to her chamber in search of her hooded cloak .... and item unused for some weeks now.

Suitably equipped for such inclemency as the morning might bestow, she set out towards the village centre. There were, in truth, two routes that Nell might take to Giles' farm: the more scenic, past Boyes Farm, down the steep hill, and up the other side of the valley to Downstead, and then straight on to Morestead .... or she could walk through the village, turn left down Crabbe's Hill to Owslebury Bottom, and then again, it was straight ahead for Morestead. There was little to choose between them, but with an eye to the weather, Nell preferred the village route, as throughout it's length, there were far more opportunities for shelter, if the need arose. She might also have the pleasant advantage of exchanging greetings with friends and acquaintances in the village, but needs must not tarry excessively, or she would miss the breakfast that had been promised her.

In reality, her father's predictions proved remarkably accurate, and as she climbed the hill from the valley of Owslebury Bottom, the sun appeared, and she was soon able to cast off her cloak.

She looked towards Morestead Church as she passed it, but it was quiet and deserted in the morning sun. She had now but to turn onto the Hazeley road, and look to the farm entrance, just a hundred yards further on her left. She paused to check her appearance, took a deep breath, and strode confidently into the farm yard.

Giles had been watching for her arrival. He was talking to the head carter, in the entrance to the barn, when she appeared.

"Good morning Nell", he called. They met in the middle of the yard, and he bowed to her very formally, before taking her arm, and escorting her towards the farm house. He was obviously delighted that she had agreed to the meeting, and seemed generally to be in the most excellent of spirits.

"I feared the notice might be far to short for you", he said, as he opened the farm house door, "but here you are .... and not too much wearied by your walk, I hope".

"Indeed not", said Nell. "It has been most pleasant to have respite from my normal Monday morning tasks around the Inn".

"And your father is well, I trust", said Giles.

"He is very well, I thank you", said Nell. "He sends his greetings, and hopes that we may soon have the company of your presence in the Inn. You seem to have forgotten us of late".

Giles laughed.

"Cares of the farm, I'm afraid Nell", he said. "But perhaps, if all goes well with my plans, I soon may be afforded a little more leisure to enjoy the company of friends over a quart of ale".

"We shall look forward to that time", said Nell.

"Indeed", said Giles, "It is with regard to this very issue that I have invited you to visit this morning".

"I'm sure I cannot imagine what you mean", said Nell.

"I hope soon to enlighten you", he said, "but first to our breakfast .... and here it is on the table".

A great pine table stood in the middle of the room. It had been furnished with a linen table cloth, and bore a new loaf, butter, a joint of ham, a bowl of eggs, and a jug of creamy milk.

Giles drew up a chair for Nell, cut the loaf, and laid two slices of ham on her plate.

"Help yourself to the eggs", he said. "They are fresh laid, and boiled not five minutes hence".

He went to the fireplace, and returned with a tall copper pot.

"I have made some coffee", he said. "Is that agreeable, or would you prefer a light ale".

"Coffee would be most agreeable", said Nell. "It is a treat I seldom have opportunity to enjoy".

For the next ten minutes they ate peacefully, finding simple enjoyment in exchanging various items of village news .... both recognising that matters of greater import would follow at the appropriate time.

They finished their breakfasts, Nell expressing much satisfaction with Giles' catering .... and then, as though to signify that the much anticipated discussion, regarding affairs of business, was about to begin, they drew back their chairs from the table.

Giles took a deep breath, and waved his arm to encompass the room in which they sat.

"With a woman's eye for domestic efficiency, Nell", he said, "I have little doubt that you have observed that even in this room all is not as it should be".

Nell looked around. The room was pleasant enough, but desperately in need of sweeping, and dusting, and much tidying .... the problem with this latter being that there appeared to be no clear decision as to the role of the furniture. Nell could not determine if she sat in an office, a kitchen, or a reception room, such was the scene around her. Every available surface was covered with an astonishing confusion of papers, and journals, kitchen ware, gardening tools, outdoor clothing .... and even, as Nell observed with some alarm .... various examples of veterinary equipment. Indeed, she and Giles sat on the only two empty chairs .... and Nell could hardly resist the temptation to suspect that the chairs had only recently been restored to their correct purpose in anticipation of her arrival.

She looked at Giles, and smiled.

"Some re-establishment of order would appear to be urgently needed", she said.

"It is the same in other areas", said Giles. "The kitchen garden is in a parlous state, the poultry are in chaos, and the dairy in confusion".

"And perhaps I should not enquire as to the conditions prevalent in the kitchen, the pantry, and the scullery", said Nell, again glancing around her.

"I would rather you resisted", agreed Giles, his face clearly portraying his dismay when he considered those offices of domesticity.

Nell laughed at his discomfort.

"I see clearly Giles", she said, "that you are in desperate, and urgent need of a good wife .... but I needs must warn you that I cannot accept such a proposal, should you have thought to invite me to breakfast with the intention of taking to bended knee before me".

Giles laughed.

"Oh Nell", he said, "I am well aware that I have no prospects with regard to winning your affections and your heart. You have made this clear to me before now. But if I have no hopes in those directions, I wondered if I might persuade you to accept a salaried role in the management of the home affairs pertaining to the farm.

Nell did her best to appear astonished.

"And you think me capable of such a role", she asked.

"I have no doubts as to your capabilities", said Giles. "With perhaps the exception of the dairy, your duties will not be so very different to those you perform at your father's tavern .... and with regard to the dairy, it is only overseeing and direction that is required. The dairy maids are skilled in their activities .... and whilst it is possible that you may be called upon for your assistance in busy periods, they will always be happy to share their knowledge with you".

Nell sat quietly, as though trying to absorb this unexpected vision of her future. Eventually she raised her head.

"Please show me around the areas of my future operations, Giles", she said. "I would like to be able to judge the scale of the task".

"Then you will consider acceptance", asked Giles.

Nell stood.

"Pending an inspection", she said, " .... and I am truly fearful of what I am about to be shown, if this room presents a standard to judge against".

FIFTEEN

For the next hour Nell toured the kitchen garden, the poultry accommodation, the dairy, and such offices around the farm yard as would be her domain. Leaving what she suspected might prove to be the worse, until the last, she insisted upon a visit to the scullery, the pantry, and the kitchen. In these cases, however, she was pleasantly surprised. Things were not perhaps quite as she would desire them, but their overhaul could sensibly be delayed until the more pressing matters in other areas had been attended to.

"I have prevailed upon the dairy maids to lend their assistance here", explained Giles. "They have been very co-operative in answering my request for help, but it has inevitably led to some disarray in their normal domains".

Nell stood looking around. She observed that here, as in all other areas, things were well found, substantial, and well conceived. It was only a lack of management and oversee that had led to the regrettable conditions so prevalent in each department.

They returned to their seats at the farm house table, and Giles made a second pot of coffee.

"Oh dear", said Nell, "The reasons for your invitation are most painfully obvious".

"Then you will accept the post", asked Giles, leaning forward in his chair with some excitement.

"Giles", she replied, "We have long been friends, and I could not easily refuse you without feelings of guilt and neglect. But I would need to consult my father. I am not sure that I can be spared from the tavern".

She smiled.

"But I will admit", she said, "that a change of scene is very appealing …. and I have a strong desire to see if I can meet the challenge to my personal abilities that your problems present. I will do my best to persuade my father that your need of me is greater than his".

"Please hasten to your father then dear Nell", he said, "for even at this very hour, indeed …. even as we sit here, there are matters around home and farm that must go neglected for want of somebody to attend them".

She held up her hand.

"Just two more issues concern me", she said. "Where will I lodge .... and what salary do you offer me".

"As to your lodgings", said Giles. "there are two alternatives. You can lodge here in the farm house .... or you can share a small cottage barely a hundred yards from where we sit, with the most senior of the dairy maids. It is a warm and cosy abode .... and Beatrice will be happy to have your companionship. I have broached the matter with her, against the possibility that you might prefer that option".

Nell smiled.

"With all due respect Mr Barnes", she said, "I must indeed lodge, as you suggest, with Beatrice. I am sure that she will be a most charming housemate .... but I will also presume upon her to act as my chaperone in this unconventional arrangement between you and I."

Giles coloured a little at this.

"As for your salary", he said, "I believe we should seek the independent and impartial opinion of your friend Mary Long. I know she has experience in these matters. I have drawn up a list of your duties. Please take it to Mary and ask her to set a salary in line with what she judges to be fair to both parties. I will gladly agree to any figure that she considers appropriate for your labours".

He crossed the room to an overflowing desk, and returned with a paper.

Nell was somewhat daunted by seeing her future occupations listed line upon line, but with further consideration, she quickly perceived that her duties at the tavern would appear equally daunting, were they laid down, line upon line, in like manner.

"If you truly believe that I am up to this ......". said Nell

"I do", said Giles. "Then you will seek the blessing of your father".

"Indeed I will", said Nell, "And I would be disappointed if he did not bestow it".

At that moment a cupboard door flew open, propelled by the tumbling of three heavy ledger books obviously stacked carelessly within.

"You will need help in accounting .... I presume", said Nell.

"I cannot expect you to be skilled in matters of recording financial activity", said Giles. "Such affairs require some training .... but if you are agreeable, then I would be willing to give you some basic instruction in the subject .... perhaps sufficient to record our daily incomes and expenditures".

Nell was just about to point out that she had been responsible for maintaining the accounts at the Ship Inn, for the last three years, when there was a knock upon the door, the head carter wishing for instruction in the priority of jobs for his horses.

By the time Giles had resolved those issues to the carter's satisfaction, the issue of accounting had gone from his mind, and Nell did not think it an important enough matter to raise a second time.

Upon such tiny incidents, such curious timings of events: a moment sooner, a moment later, can the eventual outcome of great histories so heavily rely .... to the very great wonder of those involved in their enactment.

SIXTEEN

Nell and Giles had parted most amicably, he to visit his herdsman, and she to return to the village, her home .... and her father.

She saw the little church of Morestead to her left, and determined to sit for a while in its cool confines. She wished to thank her Maker for His kind benificence in this opportunity for her improvement .... and thought to petition His assistance in guiding her through those trials and tribulations that must inevitably lie in wait for her. She thought for a moment to find the door locked, but to her surprise it stood wide open, held by a wooden wedge, as though to permit ingress of the air and sunlight of what was now becoming a very pleasant afternoon. She coughed discreetly, lest there be somebody in the church who might be startled by her sudden appearance.

"Good afternoon", said a voice from within.

Nell's eyes took a few moments, coming as they had from the bright sunlight, to adjust to the interior. She found herself not in the church proper, as she had expected, but in a small anteroom which, from it's domestic furnishings, she perceived must serve as a parish meeting place for the small community at Morestead.

Sitting at the table was a young man in the garb of a parson. He rose immediately upon Nell's entrance, and smiled in welcome.

"Oh dear", said Nell, "I apologise for intruding father. I thought the church to be empty, and had intention of a few minutes quiet reflection and prayer".

The young parson frowned.

"And call no man father upon this earth", he said, "for one is your Father, which is in Heaven".

And then he laughed at Nell's discomfiture.

"I do apologise for sermonising so inappropriately", he said, "but I could not resist quoting from Matthew's Gospel".

" .... from chapter twenty three, at verse nine, if I remember correctly", said Nell.

The parson looked astonished.

"It is a pleasure to meet a young lady who knows her scriptures", he said. "Please forgive me .... may I offer you a seat at this table, or would you prefer to enter the church".

He beckoned to his left where the door stood slightly ajar.

Nell saw no harm in accepting his invitation. In fact she felt it would display a lack of courtesy on her part, if she were to refuse.

"I have been enjoying a glass of lemonade", said the parson, indicating an earthenware jug, standing on the table. "May I offer you the same".

Nell smiled at this unexpected offer of further refreshment.

"I could not easily refuse such a blessing on this warm afternoon", she said.

The parson went to a cupboard on the wall, and returned with a second glass, which he filled, and passed to Nell. They both sat.

"We must proceed with our introductions", he said. "I am Simon Johns, and as you may have supposed, I am the Minister for this parish of Morestead .... although, I must add, only very recently arrived".

"Reverend Johns", said Nell, rising to perform her curtsey. "I am honoured to have made your acquaintance".

Reverend Johns rose quickly to his feet, and bowed formally in response.

Nell smiled.

"And I am Nell Mansell, daughter of Tom Mansell, landlord of the Ship Inn at Owslebury", she said.

"Miss Mansell", said the Reverend Johns. "I am greatly honoured to meet one associated with that fine establishment".

Nell feigned surprise.

"Should one of your calling express approval of a common alehouse", she asked teasingly.

"Where a house of refreshment for the physical aspect of a man's needs is correctly managed, and has a reputation for proper behaviour amongst it's clientele, then I can see no reason for disapproval", he replied. "But come .... we must resume our seats .... and our enjoyment of this beverage".

They sat, and sipped at their respective lemonades.

Nell was quite unable to resist a further foray.

"I fear our Minister at Owslebury seldom gives us the pleasure of his company in the Inn", she said. "He sees our house as a most undesirable competitor to that which is under his authority .... but perhaps you might care to visit. I am sure my father would be pleased to serve a man of the cloth .... especially one with the enlightened views you have expressed".

The Reverend Johns laughed.

"How could I refuse such a pleasant invitation .... and so perceptively expressed", he said. "By all means .... but let me first find my feet here in the parish .... and I will certainly visit with you and your father".

"My father certainly", said Nell, "but as for myself .... I am about to take up employment, and indeed residency, in your parish, as manager for the home affairs of the farm belonging to Mr Giles Barnes".

"Then that is but two hundred yards from where we sit", said the Reverend Johns, with some excitement, " .... and I will look forward with the greatest of pleasure to welcoming you to our small congregation .... when you are quite settled in your arrangements of course".

Nell blushed.

"I'm afraid", she said, "that although I intend to be resident at my employment during the week days .... I had planned to return to Owslebury on Saturday evenings, to be able to spend some time with my father .... and (she added hastily) to be able to attend my normal place of worship at Saint Andrews on Sunday mornings".

The Reverend smiled at her.

"Then it is most fortunate", he said, "that I am about to instigate a short service of worship here in this church, each Wednesday evening, to accomodate those who find themselves in your position .... of which there are several young persons to my knowledge. For is it not a shame that those who work together for six days each week should not have opportunity to come together .... to experience that same fellowship in worship that they have enjoyed in their weekly employment".

Nell saw that she was well and truly beaten. For the briefest of moments she entertained a most uncharitable thought: namely that the concept of a Wednesday evening service had no lengthier history in the Reverend Simon Johns' mind than that moment when she had expressed the proposal to return to her home on Saturdays. A most uncharitable thought. She dismissed it immediately .... but not without considerable surprise at her own vanity.

"In that case", she said, "I would be delighted to attend on Wednesday evenings .... and who knows that I may be able to presume upon my fellow workers on the farm to accompany me".

"Ah .... I perceive you have no intention of being made to suffer alone", said Simon Johns .... much amused at Nell's shocked expression.

"Miss Mansell", he said. "I beg of you .... fear not. The service will be of but short duration, and I hope to be able to provide some simple refreshment, here in this room, to follow .... so that the evening may have a social, as well as a spiritual purpose. In fact (he added) it was the presence of this small meeting room that initially inspired the concept".

Nell smiled, concealing some amusement at this final pronouncement. She must give the Reverend Johns the benefit of the doubt. He was, she need not be reminded, an ordained Minister of the Church .... and plainly one upon whom she could find herself readily able to bestow some warmth with regard to her feelings.

SEVENTEEN

The following Monday afternoon saw Nell, her friend Mary Long, and an elderly gardener named Stubbs, standing together in the kitchen garden at Morestead farm. A kitchen garden now under Nell's management. Giles had procured Mr Stubbs from the nearby village of Twyford. They stood quietly .... surveying the scene: the chaotic weed growth, the collapsed and tangled bean poles, the fruit cages invaded by brambles, and the derelict fruit trees .... all apparently un-pruned for several years.

"Late in the season to manage too much Ma'am", said the gardener. "I've tried digging in one or two places though, and there's nothing to fault with the soil. With a lad to help, we might get the fruit trees pruned in time to get a crop. Same with the fruit cages, once we have those brambles cleared, and onto a fire. And I think to get a pony plough in here to break the soil. I've seen the carter, and he's able to help us with that. Save a lot of time with a pony plough .... and a harrow afterwards of course".

"It will be too late to grow from seed, will it not", asked Mary Long.

"I'm afraid it is Ma'am", said the gardener. "But we could put in plants if we had them. I could ask around".

"No need of that", said Mary. "Our garden at the hall can supply you. I anticipated the problem here, and have already checked our situation. Our gardener will supply all you need if you draw up a list for him".

"It would certainly be a big help Ma'am", said Stubbs. "I can have the soil ready in a few days".

"Could we grow potatoes", asked Nell.

"Easiest thing in the world to grow .... if we have the seed", said Stubbs. "Sooner we get them in, the better though .... if we have them ....".

"Again .... I think we can help with that", said Mary. "We are just about to place an order with our merchant, so I will add your requirements to that, if you let me know the quantity".

73

The gardener nodded, and then smiled at the two ladies.

"It's asking a lot .... this late on", he said, "but no doubt we'll manage something if we can start soon enough".

Nell smiled at him.

"I'm sure that we may trust you to do all that you can", she said.

Stubbs touched his cap.

"I'll find a lad from the village to help, and we'll set to work tomorrow morning .... if that suits you Ma'am", he said.

"It will suit me very well", said Nell, "and I will ensure that Mr Barnes speaks to the head carter to organise the pony plough".

"I'll wish you a good day then Ladies".

Stubbs touched his cap again, and was gone, leaving Nell and Mary to discuss the planting.

"Mary", said Nell. "I must insist that you view my new place of dwelling. The cottage is quite charming, and my housemate, Beatrice, has the sweetest disposition. She has spared no pains to make me feel at home in my new abode".

Mary laughed.

"I shall certainly insist upon viewing your new domestic arrangements", she said. "Indeed I could not easily depart until I had satisfied myself that my dearest friend has all that she needs for her comfort and well-being".

Nell led Mary across the yard, to a well trodden path between the barn and the granary .... this last of fairly recent construction, against the forthcoming harvest from Giles' new arable endeavours. A group of hens, watched over by a proud cockerel, scratched happily between it's supporting staddle stones, as Nell and Mary approached.

"The poultry appear in good health", said Mary.

"They are indeed", said Nell, "But whether they are as productive as they should be, I have yet to determine. I have formed a list of priority in my mind, and I am confident that their management will fall under my scrutiny in the very near future. For the moment I must leave them to their own devices".

Mary laughed.

"I am sure that they will benefit greatly from the new regime", she said.

Another fifty yards brought them to a small, but attractively proportioned cottage, set with it's rear to some open pasture land. Giles' dairy cattle were visible in the distance. They had seen fit to seek the shade of some fine large beech trees, against the warmth of this sunny morning.

"The cottage has a kitchen and parlour below", said Nell, "and two chambers above. Beatrice offered to move from her present chamber, should I prefer the warmth of that which is over the kitchen. She is so thoughtful .... but I could not for a moment consider putting her to the slightest trouble or labour on my account, and expressed myself perfectly content to take the room above the parlour".

They entered the cottage, and Mary was pleased to see the rooms freshly painted, and generally clean and wholesome in every respect. Nell stirred the fire in the hearth, and set a kettle to boil. Mary had brought her a gift .... a small caddy of tea.

"Will you take tea", asked Nell.

"Indeed I will", replied Mary. "Am I to have the pleasure of meeting your housemate, Beatrice, do you think".

Nell smiled.

"I am sure that can be managed", she said. "If you will excuse my absence for a few moments, I will call her from the dairy .... assuming, of course, that she can be spared".

Leaving Mary to mind the kettle, Nell ran across the farmyard to the dairy. She found Beatrice, and her two assistants, washing their pans and utensils from the morning's activities.

"Ah .... Beatrice, there you are", said Nell. "Can you be spared for a few moments. My dear friend Mary Long is visiting, and is hoping to meet you. She is making tea for us in the cottage at this very moment".

Beatrice smiled at Nell. She reached up to return a copper pan, that she had been drying, to it's normal position on a shelf. She wiped her hands on her apron, and curtsied.

"Why …. thank you Miss Nell", she said. "If you will allow me just a few moments to set the girls to the butter making, and if you are both willing to receive me as I am, fresh from my morning's labours, I will be thrilled to meet your friend Mary".

Nell smiled at this. By neccessity, all operations in the dairy must be carried out to such exacting standards of scrupulous cleanliness that there was scarcely a time when Beatrice and her companions could not be presented before the King, so clean and charming were their appearance".

"Mary is looking forward to meeting you", said Nell, " …. and as to your appearance …. you are quite as clean and pleasant as anyone could wish for".

Beatrice smiled with pleasure at Nell's compliment.

"Then I will be pleased to join you in just a few moments", she said. She bobbed a curtsy, and turned to the task of instructing her assistants. Nell was just about to leave, when Beatrice called to her.

"Miss …. shall you take a pitcher of milk for the tea", she asked.

Nell laughed. She was not yet so familiar with the making of this newly popular beverage that she had thought to remember it's most vital component. Beatrice smiled at her. She reached a stoneware pitcher from the shelf, dipped it into a gleaming copper churn, and handed Nell a quart of fresh milk.

"Thank you Beatrice", said Nell. "I had quite forgotten ……… We shall receive you in a few moments then".

Nell, carrying the milk with great care, crossed the yard, shooing the hens from her path. She arrived in the cottage kitchen to find Mary lifting the kettle from the fire.

The tea having been made, they sat at the table to await Beatrice. They had but uttered a few words of conversation, when that young lady arrived. Nell immediately saw that she had removed her mob cap to allow her fine head of blonde ringlets to fall naturally about her shoulders. As Nell intoduced her to Mary, she fell to wondering: was it possible that Beatrice had drawn in the waist of her bodice a little .... for the purpose of displaying her figure ....

Intoductions completed, the three women sat with their tea. Beatrice's vitality was entrancing. She was quick to smile, even quicker of mind, and her mannerisms and movements were so utterly charming and feminine that Nell found herself quite bewitched.

"I am so pleased to meet you at last, Beatrice", said Mary. "Mr Barnes has often spoken of you .... and I believe that your sister, and my maid Gwen, are acquainted".

"Indeed they are", said Beatrice. "They are the greatest of friends".

"And is it true that you have some Scandinavian ancestry", asked Mary. "I feel I have heard Gwen mention as much".

"Yes Ma'am", said Beatrice. "My mother is Swedish. I have oftimes been told that I have inherited her blonde hair and her complexion".

Mary smiled.

"You have certainly inherited the finest qualities of your race", she said. "I was fortunate enough to visit Sweden in my youth, and I will confess that I would have recognised the traits of that people in your appearance, even had I not known of the connection".

Beatrice blushed.

"Do you not feel that we Scandinavian girls can be a little heavier in our countenance when set against the wonderful delicacy of English ladies", she asked.

Mary shook her head.

"I do not", she said. "Scandinavian beauty and English beauty are two sides of a very fine gold coin. There will be no lack of suitors to assure you of such .... when you choose to receive their compliments".

Beatrice blushed and lowered her eyes, but Nell also saw in her reaction something that she herself could scarce explain. It appeared to Nell that the blush were for some reason other than the normal female confusion .... that confusion so readily caused by a compliment received from an unexpected direction.

They finished their tea amidst pleasant conversation concerning Nell's future in managing the farm's home affairs. Mary eventually made ready to depart.

"I must return to my duties at the Hall", she said. "I have a new young mother to visit".

They all stood, and Beatrice curtsied her farewell, but Mary came to her, took her firmly by her shoulders, and embraced her warmly.

"Beatrice", she said. "I am leaving my dearest friend Nell in your loving and capable hands. Do you promise me that you will care for her as though she were your own sister".

Beatrice glanced at Nell .... who found herself blushing, without any clear understanding of why her cheeks should react in such a manner.

"I promise", said Beatrice, and she leaned forward to kiss Mary on the cheek.

"There .... it is sealed with a kiss", she said.

A few moments later, Mary had said her farewells to Nell, and had started her journey to Marwell. It was a fine afternoon for a walk .... and she had much to consider.

"Oh my dearest Nell", she smiled to herself. "How the unexpected so often arises to throw the best laid plans awry. How could either of us have forseen the part that Beatrice is want to play".

She shook her head.

"I feel Nell will have much to impart next time we meet", she thought. "But that she will be well cared for .... of that I have no doubt .... no doubt at all".

EIGHTEEN

Nell spent the first part of the afternoon in drawing up her list of horticultural requirements for the kitchen garden .... most importantly, the plants to be procured from the Hall. Her list would, of neccessity, be the subject of some discussion with Stubbs, when he returned on the morrow.

At three, Nell was called to the dairy. The weather had turned hot and sultry. A thunderstorm was in the making .... and under such conditions the butter simply would not form in the churn, though the dairy maids turned the barrel till their shoulders ached from exertion. Beatrice explained that she had dismissed her assistants for the moment, but that they would all try again to make the butter in the cooler air of the late evening.

Nell readily accepted this appraisal of the situation, quite willing to recognise that Beatrice had much knowledge and experience of those matters pertaining to the skills involved in the produce of the dairy.

There being no labours requiring their immediate attention, Nell and Beatrice returned to the cottage.

The dairy building had offered them some respite from the discomfort of the afternoon, but the farmyard was exposed to the full force of the sun, the heat, and humidity, fast becoming intolerably oppressive. Nell smiled to see the cockerel and his hens hidden deep within the shadows of the new granary, as she and Beatrice passed by.

"I fear we shall have a storm later tonight Miss Nell", said Beatrice.

Nell could only agree. As they approached the cottage, she glanced at the dairy herd, now all laid down in the lush grass .... a sure sign of a change in the weather.

The two young women sank thankfully onto the kitchen settle. Beatrice drew two cups of cool water from a moisture laden storage jar in the small pantry adjacent to the kitchen. She suddenly smiled actively at Nell.

"Would you care to bathe this afternnon Miss", she said. "We have some hours before the day cools sufficiently for me to attempt further operations in the dairy".

Nell looked up in some astonishment.

"Is it not just too warm to contemplate the trouble of drawing water from the well in sufficient quantity to fill a tub", she asked.

Beatrice laughed.

"That was not my meaning Miss", she said. "There is the most wonderful place where we might bathe not three quarters of a mile's walk from where we sit. Set in a small copse, further down the valley, there is a pool fed by a natural spring. It is perfectly quiet and secluded, and we may bathe there without fear of being disturbed by any other than the rabbits and birds that frequent it's waters".

"Will it not be cold despite the heat of the day", asked Nell. "I have been raised to fear taking a chill from the effects of bathing in cold water".

Beatrice smiled.

"You need have no fear of a chill", she said. "The great curiosity of the spring is that the water comes forth from the ground at a temperature to make the pool a very pleasant place to bathe. I have heard Mr Barnes refer to the place as a "Hot Spring". He says that the spring is responsible for the conditions that cause there to be such lush grazing in the meadows through which the resultant stream flows".

"I have never heard of this wonder, yet it is situated so locally", said Nell, with some astonishment.

Beatrice blushed.

Mr Barnes insists that the knowledge is preserved strictly within the farm staff", she said. "He fears that the place might become too popular were it widely known, and his herds disturbed from their peaceful grazing".

Nell, intrigued as she was by this proposed excursion, was somewhat cautious of it.

"I have no knowledge of swimming", she said. "I might wish otherwise .... but Owslebury, where I have spent all my life, sits on a hill top. The only water beyond that which we draw from the wells, are the few ponds around the village, and frequented as they are by cattle and ducks, they are hardly suited to bathing .... though infants may choose to wet their feet in them on occasion .... to the horror of their mothers".

Beatrice smiled reassuringly at Nell.

"The pool is only of any appreciable depth in it's very centre", she said, "You will be quite safe in the shallows where the water is barely at waist height .... but if you would care to experiment in the art of swimming, then I will be pleased to instruct you. It is the most wonderful exercise for the limbs, as any physician will confirm".

Nell shook her head.

"I have no suitable apparel for public bathing", she said. "Indeed .... I have never possessed such a thing .... again, because my village has not the conditions that would lead to such a purchase".

Beatrice laughed.

"As to that Miss", she said, "We will be both young women together, and therefore unlikely to find great surprise in each other's physical conditions.
I have no shame of the form in which my Maker chose to create me. Indeed .... do you not feel the same regarding the matter".

Nell smiled. Beatrice's arguments were difficult to reproach.

"Then we will go", she said.

"After all", she thought to herself. "What right have I to prudery, when my recent history is considered ....".

....

Nell and Beatrice adjourned to their respective chambers to make such preparations as were neccessary for their bathe. Beatrice had suggested that they would find it most convenient to wear non but their shifts to the pool .... their bodices hardly being practical for such a visit. Nell prepared herself according to these instructions, and donned her long hooded cloak that she might make the journey without raising comment from any persons that they might encounter. Returning to the kitchen, she found Beatrice similarly garbed. That young lady had fetched towels from the linen chest, a blanket from the closet, and had put together a flagon of elderflower presse and some fresh bread and cheese into a basket that they might not lack sustenance following their bathe.

Notwithstanding the heat, the two young women set out joyfully .... although, should Nell have bared her feelings completely, she must needs admit to some disquiet in her disposition. She had (and preferred to set the thought aside) known Beatrice for but a few hours .... indeed, since arriving to take up her new duties at the farm that very morning. This excursion was such that her normal reserve with others, whatever their sex, was likely to be thrown into disarray. She must take a deep breath .... and suit her actions to the moment. She certainly wished to spare Beatrice any concerns for her well being and composure .... whatever might befall.

Beatrice led them across meadows rich with wild flowers. Nell must have identified no less than two score of differing butterflies before they reached the outskirts of the copse that Beatrice had mentioned. Again, she led Nell around it's outer limits, before they were able to take a path to it's inner sanctom.

They came out of a stand of birch trees, and Nell gasped in wonder at the beauty before her. The pool itself was some forty yards in diameter, virtually circular in form, the grass running all but to to the water's edge. The water was perfectly clear, Nell able to view clearly the bottom composed of chalk, and coloured shingle. Set back amongst the low bushes were such a variety of wild blooms that Nell could only assume that the warm water encouraged their abundant presence in this spot .... where surely they must have failed only a furlong distant.

Her reverie in the beauties around her was started by a splash, and she turned to see that Beatrice had entered the pool. She had divested herself of both her cloak, and her shift, and now stood just as she had entered this world, beckoning Nell to join her.

Nell coloured. It was obvious that she had little choice but to follow suit if her companions natural and innocent actions were not to be thrown into question.

Reminding herself, once more, that she had no right to modesty in such a situation, she unfastened her cloak, and laid it with the basket and towels on the grass. Her shift defeated her however. Her hands would not obey her, and she coloured in confusion.

Beatrice, spying her predicament, came to her aid. She came laughing from the water, confronted Nell, and simply and swiftly pulled the troublesome shift over her head.

"Oh Nell", she said, "I must apologise to you. I had quite forgotten your natural

English hesitancy in removing your clothing. But you will soon loose your reserve when you begin to enjoy the pleasure that the water can bestow. Come with me now, and if needs must, then you can submerge yourself until you become more familiar with your condition".

With that she took Nell's hand and led her into the pool until the water was at waist height. As though to show example, Beatrice submerged herself till only her head was visible. Nell followed suit, and the two young women laughed, and stirred the water with their palms, and smiled at each other, whilst Beatrice chatted away happily, until she discerned that Nell's inhibitions had abated.

With Nell now plainly enjoying her bathe, Beatrice exhibited her skills in swimming. She carried out a circuit of the pool, her movements displaying such effortless grace, that Nell, watching enviously, could only determine that she would master this new activity, even if she must, by neccessity, risk drowning in the attempt.

Beatrice returned to her, emerged laughing from the water, kissed Nell on the cheek, with cool lips, and laid her hands on Nell's shoulders.

"Now Nell", she said. "Beatrice will make a swimmer of you. And if we will swim .... we must first grow used to being submerged".

And with that, she pushed Nell's head beneath the surface, and joined her there.

NINETEEN

The rest of the afternoon was a delight to Nell. She applied herself diligently to Beatrice's instruction, and some two hours later, with much encouragement from her tutor, surprised herself by managing some two dozen strokes quite unaided. She had not quite the courage to attempt a crossing of the pool, fearing the depths at it's centre, but Beatrice expressed herself astonished that Nell should progress so rapidly in an activity so unfamiliar to those who have no access to suitable water.

Nell had been a little troubled at first by Beatrice's frequent physical touch, but had decided that it must, for the purpose of her improvement, be neccessary. She could understand that the position of her body, and the actions of her arms, and legs, must constantly be corrected, if this new activity were truly to be mastered. As the session had progressed however, Nell had grown pleasantly familiar with the gentle touch of her lively young companion, and must admit that her own eagerness to please had spurred her to greater effort than she might otherwise have managed.

As they dried themselves, whilst enjoying some of the bread and cheese from the basket, Nell could only wonder that little more than two hours had passed since she had exhibited such inhibitions in the company of her new friend, that the simple action of removing her own shift had been quite beyond her ability to manage.

"How readily", she thought to herself, "do we grow familiar with new experience, when we have a willing companion to guide us. A companion to perceive that we have hesitated through fears that are quite unwarranted".

Having dried themselves, they folded their wet towels into the now empty basket, drank the last of the presse from the flagon, and set out on their return to the farm. The afternoon, turning now into early evening, remained dry. As they crossed the final meadow, the first stirrings of a breeze ended the sultry heat of the day, and Beatrice expressed a hope that the butter might yet be churned successfully.

....

After calling briefly at the cottage for the purpose of reinstating more habitual garb for their duties, Beatrice returned to the dairy, and Nell decided on a visit to Giles, that she might hear of his successes, or perhaps his tribulations, at the market.

She found him at the table where they had breakfasted but a few days previously. He looked up and smiled as she entered.

"Well my dearest Nell", he said. "Are you yet settled in. Are the hens laying to order, the butter obediently churning, the garden vegetables standing proudly to attention, and our store rooms a model of organised provision".

Nell curtsied, and laughed.

"My dear Mr Barnes", she said. "You surely expect great things of me .... but must I remind you that I did not arrive until eight o'clock this morning, and scarce had Beatrice shown me to my quarters, when it was time to meet with Stubbs the gardener, and Mary Long from Marwell Hall. I have indeed introduced myself to the poultry, and the hens have been made aware of their new productivity targets, but as for the butter, we are delayed ....".

"Ah yes", said Giles. "Thundery weather wreaks havoc in the smooth running of the dairy".

"Beatrice is there now .... attempting again to churn the butter", said Nell.

"She is always mindful of her duties", said Giles. "And how do you find her as a housemate. Has she done all that she can to make you feel at home".

Nell turned away that Giles might not see a colour rise to her cheeks.

"She has indeed", she said. "We are likely to become close friends. She has the most pleasant disposition".

"She does" agreed Giles. "But mind .... her Scandinavian blood can give rise to certain traits of character than seem strange to English sensibilities. But there .... I am sure you will accomodate her, should she take you by surprise".

Nell laughed.

"I see no troublesome burden in accommodating Beatrice in such matters", she said. "Indeed, I look forward to gaining her closer acquaintance".

"With that view then Nell", said Giles, "Please have my blessing in returning to the cottage that you and she may have an hour or two together before you retire. I am sure you have done all you could sensibly manage on your first day here".

"Thank you", said Nell.

She was just about to turn away, when she remembered ......

"Giles ....", she said.

"Yes", he said. "The pony plough. You shall have it, and the under carter at your disposal for the morning. The carter came to me about it when I returned from market".

"And you fared well at market", asked Nell.

"Why thank you Nell .... I fared very well. The farm is safe from the baliff for the rest of the week. Of that I can assure you".

He burst our laughing at Nell's shocked expression.

"Out with you Nell", he said. "Ask Beatrice to share her stories of butter making in Sweden. You will learn much of interest from her, I have no doubt".

"Goodnight Giles", she said.

She turned back again.

"Giles" she said. "I will do all that I can to prove my worth to you ;... I promise".

He stood and shooed her to the door, as though she were an errant hen.

"To your rest now", he said. "Before I see fit to carry you there".

Nell laughed, picked up her skirts, and ran.

....

She had the fire burning brightly, and the kettle singing on the trivet, when Beatrice came in from the dairy.

"We have the butter made at last", she said. She sank on to the settle.

"I cannot tell which has made me most pleasantly wearied: my exertions this afternoon at the pool .... or the butter churning".

She laughed.

"Did you enjoy your bathe today Nell", she asked.

"Very much", said Nell. "Are you prepared to continue with my instruction in the art of swimming".

"With the greatest of pleasure", said Beatrice. "It brought me great satisfaction to see you improve so rapidly".

"I am sure it was due to my firm but gentle coaching in the art", said Nell. "You are a skilled teacher .... that is plainly apparent to me".

"It is the loveliest occupation to share knowledge with those interested to learn", said Beatrice. "My mother had great hopes of my entering the teaching profession, but my father died quite unexpectedly, and we came to England so that she could be with her sister. It soon became obvious that England has little use for female teachers, although it is the norm in Sweden".

Nell smiled at her.

"I will mention your skills in instruction to my friend Mary Long", she said. "She has connections in many quarters, and it may be that she could assist you in your ambitions".

Beatrice sighed.

"Oh .... I am now quite happy as a dairy maid" she said. "It has it's challenges, as you have seen today".

Nell heard her words, but the wistfulness in her expression belied them.

She went around the table to Beatrice, and kissed her on the cheek.

"I will speak to Mary", she said. "She can be extraordinarily resourceful where other's welfare is concerned .... as many on her father's estate will testify".

Beatrice sighed again.

"It would be lovely Miss", she said, "But for the moment it seems that the Good Lord has sent me the most willing of pupils .... and with that I am well contented. Indeed, I have so much to teach her, I scarce know where to begin".

TWENTY & TWENTY ONE

Editors note: Upon reflection, we have decided that it is quite impossible to separate these two chapters. We are firmly of the opinion that they must be read as one.

Swimming is want to bring a pleasant state of peaceful weariness to any who indulge in it's pleasures, and it was not long before Nell and Beatrice were expressing themselves as well and truly ready for their night's repose.

As they made their final preparations to retire, they were both startled by a strong gust of wind that shook the door, and rattled the windows. A few minutes later the rain began. Heavy drops against the panes, and within moments Beatrice had rushed to lay a cloth at the bottom of the door against the water that began to seep under it's lower edge.

"Don't worry Miss", said Beatrice. "A cloth usually keeps us dry within .... but I will admit that this sounds to be an exceptionally heavy downpour".

Having layed a second cloth for good measure, they covered the fire, extinguished the candles, and mounted to their chambers.

Nell reflected on the day as she donned her nightdress and brushed her hair. Although she had looked forward to the peace and solitude of her chamber, she now must accept that it was her first night in a strange house, her first night in a strange room, and her first night in a strange bed. And if those circumstances were not, by themselves, sufficient to prevent her from sleeping then, the thunder and lightning that began at the very moment she layed her head on the pillow, seemed certain to ensure that she would have not the remotest chance of peaceful repose for some hours to come.

But if she were honest with herself, she must admit that even had she been in her own bed, in her own room, and in her father's tavern .... on the most peaceful of nights, then she still could not have slept.

She realised with great wonder, that try as she might, she could not divert her mind from the events of the afternoon. Her excitement at such new experiences would allow her no peace. She thought back to the moment, indeed of her alarm, when she realised that Beatrice saw clothing as being quite uneccessary for one's modesty: that it could simply be thrown aside when practicality demanded. She thought of her painful embarassment when she realised that Beatrice expected the same of her. She now blushed to remember that Beatrice had seen her distress at this concept .... that she was quite unable to be compliant .... and had promptly helped her through the difficulty, without any compromise to her sensibilities. She considered, with pleasure, her growing confidence in the water, a medium of which she had such limited experience, and recognised that this confidence stemmed from her eagerness to acquit herself well in the eyes of her young companion.

And now, as she lay, this way, and that way, in her bed she must accept that she longed for Beatrice's touch .... to enjoy, once more, Beatrice's instruction. To experience again, that firm but gentle correction in the eager movements of her body and limbs.

She lay .... and suffered .... as she could never have imagined she could suffer, longing for the touch of one of her own sex. And she had no understanding of how this could be. Was she not a woman. Did nature not decree that her bed mate should be a man. That their differing physicality was the at the root of the attraction that led the two sexes into intimacy. She lay struggling with her feelings .... unable to account for them in any sensible way.

And as she lay there, the storm grew stronger, the lightning brighter with each flash, and the thunder heavier in it's resonance, until the very cottage seemed to shake in unison with it's reports.

Finally there came a pause. The rain abated, the thunder ceased, and the room darkened. And at that moment there came the gentlest rap on Nell's door.

Nell felt her heart pause in it's regular beat. Could it be that once again her dreams were to be answered with so little effort on her own account.

"I am coming", she said softly.

She layed aside the covers, straightened her gown, attended to her hair, and gently opened her chamber door.

Beatrice stood there. She studied Nell with such youthful hope in her eyes .... and yet uttered not one word of enticement. Nell smiled joyfully at her .... and placed her finger on her lips to indicate that speech was not needed. She took Beatrice's hands in her own, and drew her gently into the sanctuary of the chamber. She closed the door.

Beatrice breathed deeply .... waiting.

Nell kissed her on the forehead, then simply and swiftly, she pulled Beatrice's nightdress over her head. She followed suit with her own gown. The moon saw fit to cast it's light into the room. The nightgowns lay pooled on the floor, glowing silvery white in the light from the window.

Nell tentatively placed her arm around Beatrice's waist, and drew her close. She moved her arms to encircle Beatrice's shoulders, milk white in the moonlight, and drew her closer, ever closer. She buried her face in the blonde ringlets that she had so admired earlier in the day

"Are we to continue my instruction", she breathed. "What lessons have you for me tonight my sweetest Beatrice".

And then Beatrice kissed her full on the lips, and the softness and intensity of the touch were more than Nell could bear. She swooned from her passion, barely able to retain sufficient consciousness to feel Beatrice's arms around her, as she was layed gently into her own bed.

And if that bed had felt strange but an hour ago .... it now became the sweetest retreat, containing all that she could possibly desire for the loving hours ahead.

....

Three days passed before Beatrice suggested a return to the pool. She explained that swimming, being, by it's very nature, such excellent exercise, was likely to cause some fatigue in a beginner, and she did not wish to weary Nell unduly, for fear that it would harm her progress.

But on the third day following her initial lesson, Beatrice opined once again that the prevailing conditions were like to cause problems in the dairy, and that the butter would be best left until the cooler air of the evening might serve to facilitate it's production. Nell readily agreed to an excursion, and the two young women set out for the pool, garbed and provisioned as before.

Nell was somewhat surprised, when they reached the pool, to be asked to spread the blanket upon the grass, and to sit quietly whilst Beatrice went into the copse on some errand. Imagining that this was simply a matter of that young lady's physical comfort, Nell was astonished to see Beatrice emerge from the trees, a few minutes later, carrying a hazel wand which she proceeded to strip of it's bark, and then trim to a length of some thirty inches, until she held in her hands that which Nell could easily recognise as a smooth and pliant switch. Beatrice stored the knife she had used for it's preparation in the basket, then turned her attentions to Nell.

"Now Nell", she said, "When I began your swimming instruction some three days ago I was something of a stranger to you, and you therefore were on your very best behaviour in my company. You were plainly very eager to please me, and you applied yourself readily and enthusiastically …. hence your rapid progress.

Today, however, our relationship is somewhat different. I have lost the advantage I previously had …. of being a "stranger" to you. You may think to be a little more relaxed in your attitude to my instruction. You may think to presume upon my affection for you. But this I will not permit.

I am going to begin the lesson now by calling the roll. You will pay attention, and answer me promptly with the words "Present Miss Beatrice".

Beatrice took up her switch, called Nell to her feet, and called the roll …. albeit just a single name.

"Present Miss Beatrice", said Nell.

"Thank you Nell", said Beatrice. "Now before you enter the pool I must make things clear to you. For the duration of the lessons, I am to be seen as your governess. You will listen to my instructions with the utmost attention, you will apply yourself to their execution with the utmost diligence. You will speak only when spoken to …. and if you wish to ask questions, you must preface such enquiry with the words "Please Miss Beatrice". You will remember that all conversation will be restricted to our application to your improvement in the activity. Is this clear to you".

"Yes Miss Beatrice", said Nell.

"And let me also make it clear to you", said Beatrice, "that should I see the slightest signs of inattention to my instruction, or indeed, anything other, on your part, than the greatest enthusiasm, and the keenest application to your lessons, you will be called from the pool, and treated to such punishment as I might deem appropriate for your misdemeanours. Do you understand".

"Yes Miss Beatrice", said Nell.

"Good", said Beatrice. "You may disrobe, and enter the pool".

Nell dare not hesitate for a moment. She discovered, however, that some elements of her inhibitions were want to revisit her mind, especially when she realised that Beatrice did not intend to join her in the water. Nell perceived that Beatrice had deliberately caused her to suffer this small degree of embarassment with the sole objective of reinstating that advantage of the "stranger" over a new pupil.

"Nell, I am waiting to begin", said Beatrice sharply.

Nell hastily removed her cloak and shift, astonished that these few sentences from Beatrice should cause her self consciouness to return so readily. She glanced at the switch. She was far from certain that Beatrice would, in reality, apply it to her correction , but remembering all to clearly the discomfort that such application could bring, she disciplined herself to proceed, accepting that her heightened sensibilities to the new order of things must soon pass off as the lesson proceeded.

She also realised that Beatrice plainly had some experience of teaching a class. That she clearly had practise in the governance of pupils under her instruction, and Nell mentally refreshed her resolve to petition Mary Long with regard to her instuctress's future.

The afternoon proceeded most satisfactorily. Nell had been a good pupil at the village school. She took instruction readily, and her enthusiasm for this wonderful new activity spurred her to rapid progress. Only once did she come close to faltering:

Beatrice had proposed that Nell now be taught the art of swimming beneath the surface of the water, and intending that her pupil should grow accustomed to the neccessary submersion, she instructed Nell to wade out until the water was deep enough to allow her to kneel on the bottom of the pool, with her head beneath the water's surface. Nell complied, somewhat nervously, but with the reassurance of her teacher that no harm could befall her, she managed the required submersion of five seconds duration. Beatrice allowed her to recover her composure, and then required a submersion of seven seconds. Again, Nell complied dutifully, counting slowly, as she had been taught, before emerging from the water. Beatrice expressed her approval, but said she had noticed that Nell was want to close her eyes before she submerged.

"This time", said Beatrice, "I want you to keep your eyes open, and to stay under to the count of ten".

Nell obeyed. She found this new sensation somewhat startling, but trusting that she would not have been instructed so, had there been any chance of injury, she did her very best to enjoy this new experience, and broke the surface of the water only after the full ten seconds had elapsed.

"Well done Nell", said Beatrice. "You are a wonderful pupil".

It was no surprise to Nell when she was immediately instructed to repeat the proceedure, but this time she must stay submerged for fifteen seconds. And in this attempt to comply, she came perilously close to failing in her resolve to obedience in her lessons.

It had not occurred to Nell that there might be fish in the pool. Certainly, Beatrice had not mentioned such a possibility. Imagine then Nell's surprise when, some ten seconds into her immersion, a large carp swam close by, apparently viewing her with some considerable disfavour. Nell started, and began to rise, only to remember at the very last moment that variance from her lessons was strictly forbidden. She quickly submerged, pleased to see that the carp had left the immediate area, and counted a very generous additional five seconds before breaking the surface. She was somewhat nervous that Beatrice had spotted her misdemeanour, and that she might be reprimanded. She stood in the water and faced her teacher.

"Please Miss Beatrice", she said. "I was startled by a fish, and must apologise if my scalp broke the water".

Beatrice laughed.

"I thought that something of the nature you describe might have occured", she said. "I had quite forgotten to mention that there are some carp in the pool. That we did not see them on our first visit was possibly due to the splashing and disturbance caused by your initial attempts at swimming".

She laughed again.

"I am sorry Nell", she said. "Your alarm was partly my fault, and you need have no fear of consequences arising from your very natural surprise".

Nell sighed with relief.

"Please Miss Beatrice", she asked. "For how long is it possible to stay submerged".

"That is an excellent question Nell", replied Beatrice. "Most people would find it difficult to sustain submersion for more than three minutes, but a sailor friend of my father's once told me of certain pearl fishermen in the southern oceans who can regularly manage seven or eight minutes below the surface .... provided they correctly exercise their lungs in preparation for a dive to the oyster beds".

Nell expressed astonishment at this information.

"As with all things", said Beatrice, "Application, and determination, can yield extraordinary achievments .... as you yourself have shown in just the two lessons you have received".

Beatrice seemed to consider for a moment, then smiled at Nell.

"Let us terminate our lesson with a simple competition", she said. "I shall join you in the water. We shall submerge together, and each shall attempt to beat the other in the duration of the submersion. The first to rise to the surface must accept defeat in the competition, and present the other with some small gift to mark their success in the challenge".

Nell laughed.

"Are you finally to accompany me in my condition then", she asked.

"I am", said Beatrice, and without further ado she removed her clothing and joined Nell . They faced each other, and held hands.

"On the count of three then", said Beatrice.

Nell exercised her lungs rapidly in preparation. She saw but little hope of winning the challenge .... but thought, at least, to make fair attempt at the sport. It was a matter of remaining calm, and holding her nerve to the very last sustainable moment.

"And remember that you must keep your eyes open", added Beatrice. "Are you ready .... then one .... two .... three .... ".

They submerged. Nell kept her eyes open. They smiled at each other, and Beatrice tried to break Nell's resolve by allowing tiny bubbles of air to escape from her nose.

Some sixty seconds had elapsed (by Nell's own count), when, to her astonishment, Beatrice indicated her defeat, and rose to the surface. Nell stayed down some five seconds longer to place her success beyond challenge. She rose laughing to face her instructress.

"Sweet Nell", said Beatrice. "You have won, and I must find a gift for you".

She placed her arms around Nell's waist and drew her close. She looked deep into Nell's eyes, and kissed her slowly and softly on her lips.

"Is that sufficient reward", she asked. "It is all I can manage here .... but it might be that I can bestow greater favour when we are privately together".

Nell breathed deeply.

"I am in your hands", she said. "If such future favour were my further instruction .... then I am breathless with anticipation".

Beatrice kissed her again.

"Come, my dearest Nell", she said. "Enough of the teacher for today. I shall think to spend the remaining hours as your lover".

She dived below the surface and swam to the bank. Nell followed her, marvelling at the newly found skills in her young limbs .... and at the circumstance of their acquisition.

TWENTY TWO

Her first week in her new role was drawing to a close. Nell began to reflect upon her return to the tavern on the coming Saturday afternoon. She looked forward to seeing her father .... and there was Jack to consider. Nell was now very confused in mind and spirit. She wondered if she might share her adventures with her friend Mary Long .... but so new were her present conditions to her mind .... and so unexpected .... that she shrank from contemplation of such a measure. Surely Mary, even though her considerable life experience must be taken into consideration, could not hear of Nell's present circumstance without shrinking back in horrified disbelief.

What troubled Nell the most was the question of her possible unfaithfulness to Jack. Had she been unfaithful .... or had she not. She simply had no experience upon which to base her decision.

But whatever her confusions, she needs must consider, and apply herself to her role as home affairs manager of the farm. She had promised Giles her most diligent application to these duties, and she was determined to give good account of herself, whatever tribulations her personal conditions might present.

Her second morning on the farm was a busy one. She was grateful for this, in that it distracted her mind from too deep a contemplation of the night hours she had spent in Beatrice's arms. She found it quite impossible to examine her innermost feelings in respect of those joyous caresses that had been bestowed upon her, and indeed those she had bestowed, 'ere she and Beatrice had fallen asleep in each other's arms, their bodies aglow from such tender ministries as Nell could never have imagined possible.

Beatrice had been away to the dairy before Nell had risen and dressed. They had not spoken of their night together. Such words as they might share with each other concerning their feelings, must wait till they were again freed from other cares. Nell was mindful of the inscription on a pottery candlestick that stood by her mother's bed, when she was a child.

"What do these words say Mamma", Nell would ask, as she traced the raised letters with her finger tips.

Her mother would laugh, take the candlestick from Nell's hands, and trace the words with her own fingers as she read them aloud to her daughter.

"I slept, and dream't that life was beauty. I woke, and found that life was duty".

"But what do the words mean Mamma", Nell would ask.

And her mother would laugh, and say.

"Do not worry about the words my sweet Nell. Shalt understand their meaning all too soon I fear".

"All too soon", remembered Nell, as she dressed, "But where there is "duty", it must also be possible to find "beauty". Surely one did not entirely preclude the other ....".

She arrived in the kitchen garden to find Stubbs the gardener directing not one, but two, boys in the clearance of weeds and brambles, and the under carter in the throws of adjusting his pony's harness to the plough. She mentioned to Stubbs that she would like him to view her list of horticultural requirements, then, well aware that a woman could be little more than a distraction at the scene of such industry, she retreated to the kitchen, to put a luncheon pack together for Giles and Beatrice. They were, this morning, intent upon a trip to Winchester, in the hopes of obtaining a contract for the supply of dairy products, to a new hostelry shortly to open in the High Street of that city.

Giles appeared in his suit, driving his smartest turnout, and waited by the farmhouse door for Beatrice to join him. She too was dressed for the visit, in the traditional dress of a dairy maid. Nell admired her blue bodice and skirt, and the fresh white bibbed apron so closely fitted to her quite exquisite figure. Beatrice smiled at Nell .... who blushed to the roots of her hair, and had to turn quickly away, having handed the lunch pail up to those hands that had given her such delight, just a few hours previously.

Nell waved the travellers away .... and then determined upon a clearance of the farmouse "kitchen" .... if that was to be the proper description of the room where she and Giles had breafasted last week. She sighed when she studied the task before her. She was not completely convinced that the room was best suited to it's present uncertain role. There was a room next door that might be better for the purpose. The hearth was larger, but it lacked an outside door. Nell went outside.

Could she persuade Giles to finance the installation of such an entrance. She was uncertain. But whatever the ultimate decision, she needs must install some order to the chaotic conditions prevalent in every aspect of the room. She began to gather journals and periodicals together, arranged by date, and on one table, well aware as she did so, that however logically she arranged them, she must by force spend the next month explaining to her employer that it was now much easier to find a certain auction result, or a stock list, than it had been under his own system of management. She sighed. She was well aware of the fearful expression that could beset any man's countenance when the word "tidying" reached his ears.

....

William Marseille, known by his friends as Jack, and to his enemies by names quite unsuited to dignified narrative, sat alone in the roundhouse of the old mill.

It was early evening, and he had eaten a light supper in the taproom of the tavern, with Nell's father. They had sought solace in each other's company .... an activity brought about, as both well knew, by Nell's absence. Whilst it was true that her father now had reason to truly recognise the practical role she had played in the erstwhile running of his establishment .... and Jack had become sadly aware that the physical pleasures she provided in his life, were now curtailed by her absence .... both had discussed the strange lassitude that had settled upon the tavern since her departure. It was as though the very beating heart had been torn from this centre of village life.

The girls that had taken her place were doing their very best. In fact they spared no effort in their attempts to compensate for Nell's absence. It might be, given time, that their personalities would shine forth, and their sweet natures prevail .... but for the moment, Nell was missed by all. Sorely missed. It was the truth .... and all admitted it who had known her.

Jack had considered a visit to the farm .... but decided against it. This was Nell's first venture beyond the sanctuary of her home, and Jack well knew that she must be allowed every opportunity to settle to her duties, and to shine of her own account. She would, after all, be returning home on Saturday.

At first Jack had marked off the days in his account book. Now he marked off the hours. He suspected that by the morrow he would have fallen to marking off the minutes till she returned.

And so he sat in the roundhouse .... a bottle of good brandy on the table before him. He had however taken but a few sips. He was not an excessive drinker, having seen on many occasions the disastrous results it could bring to those who followed his profession.

He heard Bess whinny from her tethered position by the mill. He started up. Bess would only behave thus if the visitor were known to her master. Could Nell have returned early .... He hastily gave consideration to his appearance. He had washed, and needs must hastily don a shirt. Just a few moments later he heard a gentle knock on the roundhouse door .... but was surprised to hear no whistle in advance. Had Nell forgotten their signal so soon ....

Jack opened the door. If he had been given opportunity to contemplate a visitor other than Nell .... one who would be almost as welcome, then he would have chosen the name of the young woman who stood before him.

"Sally", he said, in complete astonishment, "What could possibly bring you here".

Such was his surprise at the intrusion, that he had to be reminded of his manners .... but minded not .... so well did he know this visitor.

"Are you able then to invite me across your threshold", she chided. " .... or do you have some doxy installed within".

Jack laughed.

"No my dear Sally", he said, "No doxy .... unless you yourself have come to apply for the role .... though I must warn you that I am now a reformed character, fully devoted to the care of one young lady whom I soon hope to make my wife".

"Yes .... Nell", said his visitor. "At least I hope that is whom you refer to".

Once again, Jack looked at her in astonishment.

"That is why you have come ....", he said..

"It is", said Sally. "Will you pour me the smallest brandy. You and I must talk. I shall not leave until I am assured of that young lady's future happiness".

Jack procured a small tumbler, and poured a little brandy into it's recesses. He passed it to his visitor, and they sat staring at each other.

"And have you told Nell the truth of your profession", she asked. "Or is she still allowed to believe that you are a highwayman".

Jack laughed.

"That profession can be a very great attraction to a young lady", he said. "Do you not remember ....".

"I am a respectably married woman", she replied, "and must needs forget ....".

"Oh Sal", Jack laughed. "Surely you have not forgotten that night on the King's business when we had no option but to share a bed for safety. You quite refused to remove your bodice, and I, out of concern for your comfort, had to insist upon it ....".

" .... and for your pains, ended up with it around your ears", said Sally. "You see why I try to forget".

They laughed. Jack poured himself a brandy, and freshened his visitor's tumbler.

"They were good times", he said. "And we achieved much. Much that could never be recognised. Much that will never be spoken of. There are people who lay safe in their beds tonight who have no knowledge that they owe their peace and repose to such as you and I".

Sally smiled at him.

"We tried", she said. "We did not always see eye to eye ....".

"I know", said Jack. "I remember the bodice. It quite spoiled the view as you prepared for bed".

"Hmmm", she replied. "You are blessed with the normal five senses, I believe. If your vision was impaired, I seem to recall that another of your senses served you well enough".

"With your permission sought .... and duly granted, as I recall the incident", said Jack.

"And as I try to forget", replied Sally. "Jack .... if ever any two people were born to be together .... with the Good Lord sensibly keeping them apart .... it was you and

I".

He laughed at this summation.

"Perhaps", he said. "Only the Good Lord, in His wisdom, could have kept us so".

"So tell me of Nell", said Sally. "Do you truly love her .... and answer me truthfully .... because her mother and mine were sisters. My mother still struggles with her loss. Nell and I are of an age. I have been sent at my mother's request to seek reassurance of your feelings towards her".

"And if you were not satisfied", asked Jack, "Would you use your craft to protect her. Would you use your craft to harm me".

"Jack", said Sally. "One of those options is readily accomplished by my arts, as well you know. The other, should it be neccessary, and there being no other recourse, would be achieved at a heavy price. More than I care to pay. Again .... as you well know. Do not cause it to end that way Jack".

He frowned.

"You have no need to worry", he said. "Place a Bible here on this table, and I will swear of my love for Nell, with my hand laid upon it".

"I have no Bible", she said. "My people swore oaths a thousand years before it's assembly".

"Then what would you have me swear on", he said.

"Oh Jack", she said. "Do you really ask that. You know it well enough".

And she took a small sharp knife from her bodice, and cut her palm, and the blood pooled on the table, and Jack placed his palm upon it, and swore his oath, and she was gone out into the night where her people lived, and still live, as they wait for their old Gods to rise in the east once more.

TWENTY THREE

Nell stood in the corner of the dairy, with her hands folded neatly in the small of her back .... as she had been taught. On a small shelf before her eyes was perched a card. The card was from a collection of a similar nature, stored in what Beatrice referred to as her "Teachers Chest". Written upon it in a neat script were the words "I must listen to my teacher, and I must apply myself to my lessons".

Nell studied the sentence carefully, making sure that her hands remained neatly folded behind her. In a few minutes (at least she hoped that it would be a few minutes) she would be instructed to return to her desk, and to write out the phrase some thirty times. She must carry out the exercise neatly, and without error, should she wish to avoid further punishment. Her task, however, was made a little more difficult, because the phrase, although simple, was written in Swedish.

Pleased that the Good Lord had seen fit to send her such a willing pupil, upon whom to practise her teaching skills .... Beatrice had proposed that she might begin to teach Nell her native language. This would be neccessary, she explained, because she was, by blood, a true Nordic Viking. She had captured an English heart, and must in due course, return with her prisoner to her native lands.

Whilst Nell could not, for a moment, imagine her father permitting her to sail away to foreign shores, she was interested to learn all that she could of Beatrice's own tongue, but soon discovered that she had no natural aptitude for this more academic study, and was want to make frequent mistakes .... hence her sojourn in the corner of the room.

She smiled ruefully to herself. It had become difficult to determine which of Beatrice's alter egos she loved the most. The sweet loving companion of her bed chamber .... or the punctiliously strict "Miss Beatrice", her teacher in swimming and Swedish.

Beatrice looked up from her own studies.

"Nell .... you may return to your desk, and commence the exercise", she said.

Nell complied, took up a quill pen, dipped it in the ink, and applied herself to her task.

Beatrice watched her with loving eyes .... and then returned to her Bible.

Nell copied the phrase carefully. She could not afford to make mistakes. The next time she was sent to the corner it would be for a full hour. It caused her some embarassment that the two trainee dairy maids were present, but Nell consoled herself with the knowledge that they too had often occupied the corner, to study their script, and to reflect upon such misdemeanour as had caused their banishment.

So far, in her lessons, Nell had received no worse a punishment from her teacher than being sent to stand in the corner, or to suffer a rap on the fingers from the switch, when Beatrice felt that her pupil's attention had strayed.

Nell wondered, without daring to ask, if Beatrice would, in reality (and should her crimes neccessitate it) punish her as Jack had done. She could scarce believe it possible, but there was quite another issue that made her unlikely to experiment with the matter.

Some days after her emotional contretemps with Jack, she had been about to bid him farewell in the mill yard. He had been ready to mount Bess, when he discovered the absence of his riding switch. Nell ran back to the mill to fetch it for him. This gave her opportunity to examine the instrument, and she was alarmed to discover that it was very capable of inflicting much greater injury than that to which she had been subjected. She realised that her membership of the gentler sex had restrained Jack in his physical chastisement of her flesh. He had ensured that her punishment would be effective, but not be beyond a level of discomfort which she could reasonably be expected to bear.

But would Beatrice exercise like restraint .... she would obviously be punishing one of her own sex .... or would she simply proceed according to the crime, with no consideration for her pupil's resilience to her ministry. Nell was uncertain .... and nervous of placing herself in a situation that would provide the answer. She bent to her work, certain that only diligent care could save her from unpleasant consequences.

....

As the milk began to arrive in the dairy (Giles' farm milked late) Beatrice took Nell's written work, and dismissed her, needing to direct the dairy in the handling of the days produce.

Nell crossed to the farm house and found Giles at his breakfast.

"Sit down Nell", he smiled. "I see you have begun to install some order in the room. Shall I ever find anything again do you think".

And he laughed.

"Do not look dismayed my dear young lady", he said. "Do you think I should employ you, only to reprimand when you enact the terms of your employment".

Nell smiled.

"I wish to discuss the room with you", she said. "It cannot be expected to serve every purpose efficiently, and with your blessing I would like to re-arrange it as an office for the business affairs of the farm".

"But what of the kitchen", said Giles in puzzlement.

"The room next door is far better suited to that purpose", said Nell. "It is blessed with a far larger hearth, a much better crane to the chimney, and even has a drain to the floor. I am astonished that it is not already in use as the kitchen .... but the lack of a door to the farm yard probably provides us with the explanation".

Giles nodded thoughtfully.

"Nell, you are quite correct", he said. "Let us examine the situation and explore the possibility of installing the required exit to the yard".

They both went outside, and by determining their location from studying the position of the windows, soon made an extraordinary discovery: that there had once been an entrance way exactly where it would be needed, were the room to become the new kitchen.

Giles pulled away the flowering creeper to expose an arched doorway that had been bricked in .... and commented that by his estimation of the weathering of the bricks, the work must have been carried out not long after the house was newly built.

"A puzzle indeed", he said. "But from a practical point of view there is now not the slightest objection, either from a constructional or financial point of view. I'm sure the work can be carried out at little more than the cost of constructing a new door to fit the opening. I shall ask the carpenter in Twyford to estimate for the works as soon as he is able to attend us".

"Then I may proceed with the reorganisation of the furnishings", asked Nell.

"You may", said Giles. "I am delighted with the proposal. We shall have a kitchen .... and an office for business affairs. Quite an excellent plan. Certainly such chaotic conditions as prevail at the moment cannot be viewed as conducive to the preparation of good sustaining meals, let alone the management of our stock and finances".

He smiled at her.

"You will be our salvation Nell", he said. "I must ride up to the sheep pastures this morning. But I shall leave all in your capable hands .... and I will endeavour to organise the carpenter".

With that, he left Nell to resume her plans .... if limited for the moment to simple sweeping, dusting, and tidying. She picked up her broom, then looked thoughtfully at the various items of veterinary equipment with which the room was littered. They must be moved .... but where now to put them ....

....

It was a peaceful morning in the home offices of the farm, and Nell progressed well with her work. She would loved to have relocated some of the furniture from the existing kitchen to the new .... but so substantial were the pieces, so heavily built, that even their slightest movement was quite beyond her power to accomplish. She could have sought help from the garden, where the carter, and gardener, or indeed the two boys could have quickly carried out her wishes, but she was reluctant to disturb them from their labours, determining that, in any case, there really was no great advantage to be gained until the new entrance was installed.

The kitchen door and windows were open to admit the fresh air of what was the most glorious morning, and occasionally Nell would hear Beatrice's voice as she instructed her assistants. On one occasion Nell winced as she heard very plainly that alarming raised tone preferred by "Miss Beatrice", on those occasions when she was dissatisfied with a pupil's behaviour.

Nell fell to considering Beatrice as a mother .... and the lot of any chidren she might have. They would certainly not lack for love .... but must mind their manners .... or indeed, "Woe betide them". And then Nell blushed as she realised that her muses were quite redundant ....

Her thoughts dwelled upon this issue. One that she had not previously considered. She had certainly looked, in the past, with some want, at those young mothers with children about their skirts, or an infant in their arms, accepting these feelings as a natural part of her transition to womanhood. Could she forsake such a future entirely. Had Beatrice considered these matters .... could the natural desires of her sex for motherhood be entirely absent from her personality. Nell struggled to imagine such a condition. And supposing that such desires might still remain there, in Beatrice's heart .... how could such a dilemma be resolved.

Nell sank into a chair, dismayed at such thoughts as she had never had cause to consider.

Her reverie was not long without interruption:

She heard horses in the yard. She had not been warned by Giles of any forthcoming visitors, indeed his expedition to visit the shepherd suggested that none were expected. She hastily examined her appearance, and straightened her cap and apron. She was alarmed to view the dust and dirt that both had collected, but she could do little to remedy her condition at such short notice, and went to the door, trusting that the visitor might forgive her appearance.

Standing in the yard was quite the most elegant carriage that Nell had ever seen. The beautifully proportioned body, resplendent in dark blue and cream paintwork, was suspended by straps from elegantly curled bearers. The compartment was fully glazed, the lights set in gleaming brass frames matched to the most ornate of carriage lamps, set on brackets to the foremost corners. Both the coach driver to the fore, and the footman in his seat to the rear, were resplendent in scarlet coats and tricorn hats, much decorated with cream lace and gold braid. The footman climbed carefully from his perch, opened the carriage door, and stood ready to offer the occupant such assistance as might be required.

Nell took a deep breath, and went forward to receive her visitor.

TWENTY FOUR

Nell was, to be truthful, thoroughly alarmed. That such a visitor was of some import was obvious, and that Giles be here to receive them, quite essential. But he had ridden off to the downland pastures and could not be expected to return for some time to come.

Nell must do her best in Giles' absence. All too aware that her appearance left much to be desired, she walked out to greet the visitor with as much dignity as she could muster. She stopped some three paces short of the ensemble, and looked to the footman. He returned her gaze somewhat haughtily.

"Mademoiselle Allouette du Chambray to visit with Mr Giles Barnes", he announced.

Nell turned to the carriage door. A young woman rose from the interior, and elegantly extended her hand that her footman might assist her in alighting. Duly aided, she stepped down into the farm yard. The footman reached up to a basket mounted by his seat, and produced a parasol, which he erected, and held over his Mistress's head.

Mademoiselle du Chambray examined her surroundings. She was rather more petite in her stature than Nell. She was expensively and elegantly attired in a richly decorated gown, the bodice so closely fitted that Nell wondered at her ability to draw proper breath. Her hair was carefully styled and laced through with ribbon to match the silks of her gown. The eye of an observer was inevitably drawn to a beauty spot on her cheek, and although Nell could admire her carefully managed appearance and complexion, there was a sharpness to the features which suggested a quick temper and an intolerant nature.

Nell smiled at her visitor.

"Good morning", she said. "I trust that you have had a pleasant journey, but I must apologise for the absence of Mr Barnes. He has ridden out to his sheep pastures, and may be some time away. Would you be prepared to wait if I could have a message sent up to him. I could offer some refreshment if you wished ....".

Mademoiselle du Chambray eyed Nell with disfavour.

"And who are you to address me with such temerity", she asked.

Nell blushed, but held her ground.

"I am Miss Nell Mansell", she said. "Manager of the home affairs of the farm, to Mr Giles Barnes".

The information was not well received.

"What foolishness is this that you speak to me of .... without so much as a simple curtsy to show your respect", she said.

In her fluster, Nell had forgotten her manners. She blushed with mortification

"I am so sorry", she said.

She executed her most subservient curtsy, and looked again to her visitor.

"I understand that Mr Barnes is not immediately available", said Mlle. du Chambray. "Would you therefore call upon his Steward, that we may discuss his summoning from whatever matters he presently attends".

Nell coloured.

"I'm afraid, Mlle. du Chambray", she said, "that Mr Barnes has no Steward, but as manager for the home affairs of the farm, I fulfil that role, and may indeed send word for Mr Barnes to inform him of your presence".

"This is impertinence of the first degree", replied Mlle. du Chambray. "I will not tolerate such absurdity. How can you claim to manage a farm. A woman must manage her coiffure, her toilette, her social connexions, her place in polite society. She has no business in managing a farm".

"Non the less", said Nell, who was now struggling to retain her composure, "my position is as I have described. Would you like me to send word .... it might be that Mr Barnes has finished his business and will be quite soon with us again".

Alouette du Chambray drew breath.

"You will listen carefully to my words", she hissed. "You will summon a person of authority. When that person arrives I will, no doubt, be able to formulate a scheme with him to ensure that Mr Barnes is made aware of my presence. And when I do have the pleasure of conversing with your master I will insist that he has you taken aside and whipped as reward for your impertinence. Had I sufficient time at my disposal I would wish to oversee the punishment, and receive the benefits of your resultant contrition ....".

It is fortunate that Nell was spared the trouble of a response to this outburst from Alouette du Chambray .... who had barely uttered the last words when the sound of hooves anounced Giles' arrival on the scene.

Nell breathed a sigh of relief. Giles dismounted and ran to join them. Nell knew him well enough to fancy that she saw a rather stricken expression about his face as he dismounted, but he was quite the composed gentleman as he approached Alouette, bowed to her, and to Nell's complete astonishment, took that lady in his arms, and kissed her gently on both cheeks.

"Alouette", he said, "You cannot imagine my joy, when I espied your equipage. Are you recently come from Paris. Why could you not warn me of your arrival that I might have been here to greet you properly. I am bereft that you treat me so. Have you news that would not wait, that I am caused such embarassment with regard your proper treatment".

Alouette held up her hand.

"Giles", she said. "I am much relieved to have the pleasure of your presence. But before we begin our discourse .... in rather more favourable conditions .... I must draw your attention to this young lady who has treated me to a display of impertinence that would cause you no little distress had you been so unfortunate as to witness the performance. She is obviously delusional, has claimed to be your manager .... and concerned for her correction, I must insist that she is subjected to a whipping from your horseman as soon as it can be arranged.

Nell saw Giles blanche.

"My dearest Alouette", he said, embracing her once again, "I am so sorry that you have been the subject of such distress. The poor girl, as you so rightly observe, is subject to delusion, and is want to claim position where she has none. It is a sad case, and out of respect to her mother we are apt to accommodate her in her delusion, whilst setting her such simple tasks around the place as are not beyond her abilities to accomplish".

"Come Alouette", he said. "Let us seek some refreshment. I will speak to the girl's mother later in the day .... but a whipping is quite unneccessary. The poor girl simply cannot be properly held accountable for her errors, I assure you".

Nell was mortified by this speech. Her complexion coloured to the brightest crimson, the tears formed in her eyes, and stripped, as she had been, of any facility to defend herself from such unwarranted condemnation, she could only turn away, and run in tearful distress to seek sanctuary in the cottage she shared with Beatrice. She sank on to the settle, and cried bitterly .... and it was there that Beatrice found her when she returned from her labours in the dairy.

TWENTY FIVE

"My dearest Nell", cried Beatrice, as she entered the room, and spied Nell's tear stained countenance. "What calamity has befallen you that you suffer such distress".

She threw her arms around Nell and began to caress her scalp, and kiss away her tears. Nell shaking with grief, buried her face in those blonde ringlets that she loved so dearly.

"Are they still there in the yard", she whispered.

"Who is it that has distressed you dearest Nell .... and who is it that you ask of".

"Alouette du Chambray", replied Nell. " .... and Giles. They are lovers, it seems".

"And it causes you such grief that they are lovers", asked Beatrice. "Can I bestow more love upon you that you are satisfied with your portion, and need feel no envy for Giles and Alouette".

Nell pulled away in distress.

"My dearest sweetest Beatrice", she said. "I am sorry for my words .... that I should have spoken so hastily and confused my meaning".

Beatrice placed her finger on Nell's lips.

"Then speak no more for the moment my sweet Nell", she said. "I thought to light the fire in the wash house earlier this morning. There will now be sufficient water to fill the large tub. Beatrice will bathe you, and wash your sweet face, and cleanse all the world's ills from your body. And while I care for you, it may be that you will be more able to express yourself calmly, and tell of what has befallen you".

She led Nell to the wash house, now pleasantly warm from the fire, and ran the contents of the copper boiler into a large wooden tub, adding cool water until she judged the temperature to be perfect for her purpose. Nell disrobed, an action now so familiar to her, that it caused her not the slightest thought or hesitancy. The water was soothing and pleasantly heated.

Beatrice bathed her, and washed her hair, and presently Nell calmed under such gentle ministry, and told her story.

Beatrice listened patiently as she soaped and rinsed. There was, by now, not an inch of Nell that she did not know, and love, more than her own flesh.

Beatrice dried Nell, and helped her don a freshly laundered night gown. Nell was to be put to bed .... whilst Beatrice sought an interview with Giles.

Nell lay in her chamber, missing the company of Beatrice, and sadly reflecting that her position on the farm seemed to be over scarce had it begun .... and to think that she had entertained such happy plans for her future.

Beatrice returned, bearing two cups of hot swiss chocolate. She smiled lovingly at Nell, and sat on the bed to tell of her expedition.

"Giles is distressed beyond measure", she told Nell. "I thought for some moments that I must minister to him as I did you ....".

She stopped to laugh at the dismay on Nell's face at her pronouncement.

"Oh dearest Nell", she said, placing her chocolate on the floor that she might embrace her friend. "I was only jesting. Such ministry is for you, and you alone, as surely you must realise by now".

Nell smiled at her.

"It seems", she said, "that my sensibilities are in a heightened state indeed".

Beatrice smiled in return.

"Be patient dear Nell", she said, "and I will explain all".

She retrieved her chocolate, and sat with Nell again.

"Giles is in every way quite as upset in his emotions as yourself", she said. "He was all for coming here to apologise immediately .... but I quite forbade the plan. He must wait patiently until your equilibrium is fully restored".

"Then is Mlle. Chambray departed so soon", asked Nell.

Beatrice shook her head and smiled.

"That young lady's departure can never be soon enough for most who know her", she said.

Nell shook her head in puzzlement.

"But I saw her with Giles", she said. "They were in embrace".

"Oh Nell", said Beatrice. "Perhaps you will look upon Giles more favourably when you know the history of their acquaintance".

Nell shook her head.

"I will find it difficult to forgive Giles for the words he spoke to Mlle. Chambray", she said, " .... though you were to petition me through the night".

Beatrice laughed happily.

"No Nell", she said, "Not through the night. I am sure that we can find happier occuption to please us".

Nell lay back on the pillow.

"I will listen", she said wearily. "Do what you can for Giles".

Beatrice finished her chocolate, and bade Nell do likewise, 'ere it grow cold.

"I have sought permission from Giles to give you some history", she said. "He could scarce refuse me once he became acquainted with your distress at his words".

She drew breath for the narrative.

"This farm is heavily mortgaged", she said. "In all but habitation, it belongs to the Chambray family who dwell in Paris. They are wealthy, with many interests in England. The introduction was made by the law firm who acted for Giles' father. There were several years of lassitude in the stock, some poor investments, and mismanagement in general .... partly caused by the illness of Giles' mother, and the strain that this placed on his father. The farm, although profitable when managed correctly, was in need of investment. The du Chambrays visited. They took up the mortgage, and so Giles was able to retain his family home. He was not happy that his hand had been forced to the measure .... but he needs must make the best of the situation. There was however an unfortunate complication, in the person of Mademoiselle Alouette du Chambray.

Her father is now of an age where he prefers to remain in Paris. Alouette loves to travel. She therefore makes regular visits to collect the mortgage payments, and to check on the well-being of her father's financial investment. She also believes herself to be in love with Giles".

"But surely nothing less than a nobleman of the highest birth would satisfy her social requirements", said Nell.

Beatrice smiled.

"Giles is a handsome young man", she said. "It is not permissable that he should not be in love with Mlle. Chambray. All handsome young men must fall in love .... they must lose their hearts entirely .... to Mademoiselle Alouette du Chambray .... or the most unpleasant consequences will ensue".

Nell shook her head in disbelief.

"And Giles is prepared to tolerate this situation", she asked, rising from her pillows.

Beatrice gently restrained her.

"He has no choice", she said. "Think of the people who rely upon this enterprise for their living. You yourself, recently arrived, I and my two maids, the carters, the shepherds, the herdsmen .... and various others. Giles is keenly aware that he has a responsibility to them all. He may no longer own the ship, but he is a good Captain, and navigates with great skill to keep us all afloat, through good times, and bad".

Beatrice paused.

"There Nell", she said. "Are you perhaps more able to restore Giles to your commendation, now that you have heard his history and appreciate his position. He takes his responsibility to us all very seriously. Will you still condemn him my sweet Nell".

TWENTY SIX

Beatrice had organised an interview with Giles for the following morning. She accompanied Nell to the farmhouse, where they found a young carpenter measuring for the new door.

Giles came straight to Nell, and took her hands in his own.

"My Dear Nell", he said. "Can you ever forgive me".

Nell smiled.

"I do forgive you Giles", she said.

"And Beatrice has advised you with regard to our situation here", he asked.

"She has", said Nell, glancing toward her housemate.

"And we can resume our affairs with no harm ensuing", asked Giles.

"We can", said Nell.

She took a breath.

"But where pray is the lovely Mlle. du Chambray .... and is she likely to return. I do not wish to risk a whipping from your carter, Mr Barnes".

"I imagine, Mr Barnes", said Beatrice, "that there was never the remotest possibility of Nell recieving a whipping from anybody .... least of all the carter".

Giles smiled at her.

"Not the slightest possibility", he said. "Of that I can assure you both. And as for Alouette .... well aware, as she is, that our primitive conditions of habitation here are quite intolerable to one of her noble sensibilities, she has removed to the comfort of the coaching inn at Whiteflood some two miles distant".

"She has removed to "The Flood"", said Nell in astonishment. "That house has little reputation for comfort, surely".

Giles laughed.

"It is indeed far more comfortable here", he said, "but in that house there will be many more people for Mademoiselle to admonish as regards their lack of manners, and breeding. And the more good souls that dear lady can instruct regarding their inferiority to her own situation, the greater in her personal superiority she must naturally appear".

"At least .... in her own estimation", he added.

Nell and Beatrice smiled. Giles continued to hold Nell's hands in his own.

"I am so glad", he said, "that we may resume our previous relationships. I look forward so much to seeing the home affairs of the farm continue to develop successfully. As you can see we are soon to have our entrance to the new kitchen, and I imagine that there will be further innovation from your direction. And of course, I am so pleased that you and Beatrice appear to have established an excellent working relationship".

Nell felt herself likely to colour at this final pronouncement, but kept her eyes demurely averted. How, she wondered, is Beatrice managing the control of her own complexion.

She was confident, however, of that young lady's composure being such as to prevent the slightest betrayal of her innermost feelings via the medium of her countenance.

"Beatrice", said Giles. "We must adjourn to the dairy. You will be pleased to learn that I have received favourable instruction from the new hostelry in Winchester. You and I must discuss their requirements, and plan that they might be met efficiently".

Beatrice and Giles left Nell to continue her work in the farm house. Nell went outside with a glass of presse for the young carpenter, who accepted the refreshment enthusiastically. Nell thought to question him regarding the matter that had so puzzled both she and Giles on the previous day.

"Are you able", she asked him, "to provide an explanation as to why this doorway was bricked over, apparently so soon after the building was constructed".

The young man smiled.

"I might offer an opinion Miss", he said. "Might I be allowed to examine the inner side of this wall".

Nell led him through the existing kitchen into the further vacant room. He examined the wall, and then the hearth, then went to the doorway that gave access between the two rooms.

"If you look closely Miss", he said, "You will see that this inner door was cut through a sound wall. I would propose that this was done at the same time that the door in the outside wall was bricked over".

"Then what is the explanation", asked Nell.

The young carpenter looked around him again.

"I imagine Miss", he said, "that this building was originally conceived as two separate dwellings .... each with an entrance doorway in the front wall. Not many years later, it became a single dwelling, the connecting door was installed between these two rooms, and the second front entrance, no longer being required, was bricked in".

Nell nodded her head slowly.

"Thank you", she said. "I think you have provided a perfectly sensible solution .... I am grateful".

"A pleasure Miss", said the young man.

He finished his presse, and placed the glass carefully on the table.

"I shall return to the workshop now Miss", he said. "I will start construction of a new door and frame tomorrow, and when they are ready, we shall endeavour to open up the doorway and complete the installation in a single morning. That should cause you the least possible inconvenience".

Nell expressed herself pleased with the plan,

"Would you be able", she asked, "to build new accommodation for our poultry. Their current conditions are most unsatisfactory".

"I would certainly be pleased to estimate for the work", he said. "Have you a design that I might view".

"I shall consult with Mr Barnes", said Nell.

The young man touched his cap, promised to return as soon as could be managed, and left Nell to examine the rooms in the light of her new knowledge.

The carpenter had not long departed when Giles came in to collect a small cotton sack.

"I must ride up to the pastures again Nell", he said. "The shepherd has need of further raddle. I shall return via the arable land to check on the oats, so I may not see you again today. It is your intention to return home this evening, is it not".

"If that is agreeable to you", she said.

"Perfectly", said Giles. "It was part of our arrangement. Would you be so kind as to carry my best regards to your father .... and indeed to Mary Long .... if you should encounter that good lady".

"Indeed I will", said Nell. "I shall return bright and early on Monday morning".

"Then I trust that you will have a pleasant break from your labours Nell", he said, "And we shall look forward to your return on Monday".

He had scarce reached the door when he had a thought. He turned back into the room.

"Nell", he said. "I promise that there are no visitors to trouble you this afternoon ....".

She made to throw a pan at him.

He laughed, and was gone, leaving Nell to consider how she might best occupy her time till she must leave for her home.

The cupboard containing the ledger books caught her eye, and she determined upon their study in the hopes of gaining clearer insight into the financial affairs of the farm, particularly in the light of her new understanding of the prevailing, if regrettable, conditions.

She poured herself a glass of presse from the flagon in the larder, cleared a space on the table, and sat comfortably to commence her explorations.

The afternoon remained a peaceful one. The first of the ledgers dated back five years, and Nell soon discovered that one book followed another, all being arranged in the normal chronological order. As she had expected, the incomes and expenditures in the day to day running of the farm were recorded in facing columns. These columns were totalled at the end of each calendar month to give a resultant profit, or loss for that month. Nell was surprised that the dairy's income was listed as a single transaction at the end of each week. She concluded that the individual sales must be recorded in a "day book" maintained in the dairy itself. She would ask Beatrice about this.

Overall, Nell was pleased to discover that the farm was indeed very well managed. Yes .... inevitably, and according to the seasons, some months resulted in a loss, but when the year end figures were examined, there was little to cause concern. The farm was profitable, with the sheep, and the dairy, providing the most reliable, and regular, income.

As her studies progressed, however, Nell became puzzled that the mortgage, and it's ensuing payments were not apparently recorded in any way that she could discover. Laying the large ledgers aside, she returned to the cupboard to see if there were another book retained for the purpose.

She quickly found a fourth ledger .... somewhat smaller than the others .... and she sat down to study it's contents, certain that this would record the outgoings that she had not yet been able to account for.

Some thirty minutes later, Nell closed this book, sat staring thoughtfully at it's cover, then returned it, with the others, to their place in the cupboard.

She was puzzled. She could go no further into matters without some explanation. And as she sat there, she remembered the uneasiness that Giles had displayed when, during their initial discussions regarding her employment, she had asked if he might require her help in maintaining his accounts. She reflected now upon that uneasiness. It perhaps made her reluctant to quiz Giles until she had a greater degree of understanding concerning what she had seen. But how to obtain such understanding, was presently beyond her ability to imagine.

TWENTY SEVEN

Nell now had two distinctly differing matters to trouble her conscience. Her most recent, regarding the farm accounting .... and, of even greater import, the dilemmas concerning her personal relationships. The former must, for the moment, be put aside. She had little idea of how to proceed. But the latter she had managed to give some thought to, and in desperation, had, as her mother had often taught her, turned to her Bible.

There was one passage that she felt might provide her with assistance .... but she needs must make further enquiry regarding the detail contained in the scripture. She therefore determined upon a visit to that recently arrived incumbent at Morestead Church .... her new acquaintance .... the Rev'd Simon Johns.

With this in mind, she hastened to the dairy to bid her farewells to Beatrice. Perhaps we will allow these two young ladies some privacy for their first parting. It is little more than they have earned.

Aware that she was leaving her duties rather earlier than might reasonably be expected, Nell intended to account for the matter with Giles on Monday, offering to work the hours that she had taken to herself. She suspected, however that once Giles understood that the time was to be spent under the guidance of the Minister, then he would simply waive the matter aside.

Nell collected the few belongings she would need from the cottage, and set out for Morestead Church.

It was Saturday afternoon, and Nell was much pleased to find the Rev'd Johns, once again sitting at the table in the church meeting room, absorbed in the preparation of his sermon for the following day.

He looked up in surprise as she entered.

"My dear Miss Mansell", he said. "I am delighted to see you again so soon. Does your new employment go well. You have not been the subject of too many tribulations, I hope".

Nell smiled.

"No, Rev'd Johns", she said. "All goes well. There was one small issue that grieved me very much, but matters have now been resolved to the satisfaction of all parties, and I am looking forward to returning to my duties on Monday".

"Ah", he said, "You are returning home, of course .... I remember that was your plan. Well I am bereft that we shall not have you as part of our small congregation tomorrow, but our loss must be Saint Andrews gain".

Nell smiled.

"Perhaps", she said, "I am no great gain for any Church assembly, should my sins be taken into account".

The Rev'd shook his head.

"Miss Mansell", he said. "I am shocked that one whom I felt to know her scripture so thoroughly is not aware of the passage that tells us that there will be more rejoicing in the Kingdom of Heaven over one sinner come to repentance than over ninety nine righteous souls".

Nell laughed.

"Rev'd Johns", she said. "You are want to give me hope".

"And where there is life, there is eternally hope", said the Reverend. "Now Miss Mansell, pray be seated. I percieve that pleasant though the company of a clergyman might be, it is hardly likely to keep a young woman from her home and loved ones, except that she should seek guidance over a matter that troubles her deeply".

Nell blushed.

"You are correct in your assumptions Reverend Johns", she said. "Have you the time to assist me or ....".

The Rev'd Johns held up his hand.

"Miss Mansell", he said. "Where a troubled soul is in need of spiritual guidance, then I must needs make the time. That is the duty and calling of this cloth".

He indicated his cassock.

Nell smiled. She was again reminded of her mother's candle stick.

"We must share a lemonade", said the Rev'd Johns.

He procured glasses and a flagon, from the cupboard, and poured two measures.

"Thank you", said Nell. She sipped at her lemonade, and frowned.

"It is concerning a piece of scripture that I had hoped to consult you", she said. "Are you familiar with the Gospel of John at chapter eight and verse three".

The Rev'd Johns closed his eyes, and thought.

"Ah .... yes indeed", he said. "The story of the woman taken in adultery".

He looked at Nell thoughtfully.

"Oh dear", he said. "I trust that your enquiry regards a truer understanding of the scripture and not ....".

"It does, Reverend Johns", said Nell hastily.

"I am much relieved", he replied. "Please continue and I will endeavour to assist you in your confusion over the piece".

"What is then meant by the term "adultery", asked Nell, "and has it's meaning changed in any way since the passage was first written".

Simon Johns took a deep breath.

"I cannot see that the meaning of the word has changed", he said. "But the way we view the transgression .... why yes .... I feel that has changed. Certainly in our society we would not put to death for the act".

"And it's meaning", asked Nell.

The Rev'd Johns looked a little uncomfortable with the question, but perceiving that his companion was most seriously interested in the scripture, he answered as simply as he might.

"The same as ever", he said. "Intimate relationships between a man and a woman outside of the confines of marriage".

He thought he saw the slightest signs of relief in Nell's response, but held his peace.

"Does this help you", he asked.

"It does", she said. "But I have further questions".

The Rev'd Johns held his palms to indicate that he was happy to receive her enquiries.

"Does Jesus forgive the woman", asked Nell.

The Rev'd Johns was astonished.

"Nell" he said. "I begin to percieve that your study of scripture goes far beyond what might be expected of one of your age and sex. That is a most remarkable question. Most remarkable".

He sat looking at her in some wonder.

"Have you considered taking Holy Orders", he asked, smiling.

"I am a woman", said Nell.

"And so were various of Jesus' associates", said the Rev'd. "But I apologise for digressing. What do you feel yourself on the issue. I am most interested".

Nell sat thinking.

"I feel that Jesus uses His quick wits to rescue the woman from execution", she replied, "But does He really forgive her. Of that I am uncertain".

"Let me refresh my memory of the piece", said the Rev'd Johns. He went through to the Church proper, and returned with a Bible. He leafed through .... and sat reading the piece.

He looked up.

"Jesus has not yet died on the cross", said Nell, "so the woman cannot yet be forgiven by His sacrifice alone".

Rev'd Johns stared at her.

"That is correct", he said.

"Does Jesus see no sin in what the woman has done", said Nell, "Or does He simply not see her sins as worthy of death, and therefore uses His wits to rescue her".

The Rev'd Johns shook his head.

"Miss Mansell ....".

"Please call me Nell", she said.

"Are you aware Nell", he said, "that this passage was omitted entirely from the first assembled Bibles".

Nell shook her head.

"By that omission", said the Reverend Johns, "We may judge that the passage has always been the subject of question".

"Can you answer the question", said Nell.

The Reverend Johns sat thinking. He drew breath.

"My opinion is this", he said. "In our present condition Jesus has indeed suffered and died on the cross that our sins might be forgiven .... and I cannot see but that must surely include the sin of which we speak".

"And of the woman in front of Jesus", asked Nell.

The Rev'd Johns smiled at her.

"If the Son of God has not the power to forgive", he said, "then who could we look to. I believe He forgave her. His final words of admonition suggest the same".

"Go forth, and sin no more", said Nell thoughtfully.

She made to rise.

"Have I served to assist you", asked the Rev'd Johns.

Nell nodded.

"Thank you", she said. "I have taken up too much of your time".

"It has been time well spent", said the Rev'd Johns. "Well spent indeed. I have enjoyed our discussion".

Nell curtsied.

"Have you yet instigated your plan for a Wednesday evening service of worship", she asked.

Rev'd Johns smiled.

"I have", he said. "May we expect your attendance".

"Pending my employers permission", said Nell, "I will be delighted to attend .... and I hope to ask a friend to accompany me".

"Wonderful", said the Rev'd Johns. "I trust that you will enjoy the visit to your home .... and that we may see you safely returned to us on Wednesday".

"Though I am a sinner ....", asked Nell.

"There is more rejoicing ....", said the Rev'd Johns.

He saw Nell to the door. He stood watching her as she walked away up the sunlit road.

"A most remarkable young lady", he said to himself. "Most remarkable indeed".

TWENTY EIGHT

Nell ran joyfully up the steps at the front of the Ship Inn. The tap room was enjoying that quiet period before the evening customers arrived. Nell's father was polishing the copper ale jugs. They had not needed to be polished, having received the same attention from Anne and her helpers only the day before. But the endeavour gave him reason to remain where he might greet Nell upon her arrival.

"Nell", he cried, as she entered the room.

He came from behind his barrels and opened his arms to embrace his daughter.

"You have been sorely missed Nell", he said, as he held her.

She kissed him on the cheek, and laughed.

"Father", she said. "Do not tell me that Anne and her helpers cannot do everything that I did. My duties were not so difficult that I might not be easily replaced".

"Oh my dearest Nell", he said. "It is not your labours that we have missed, but your presence amongst us, to lighten our days, and to keep us on the narrow road to salvation".

Nell laughed.

"I surely am the least likely to accomplish such a task", she said, "Even were it needed .... which I doubt".

"Will you sup with me Nell", he asked, "or have you some urgent errand that cannot be delayed".

He said this last with a smile.

"All three of the girls are here to manage the tap room, whilst you and I may have the parlour quite to ourselves".

"I could not consider any other plan", said Nell. "What supper have you prepared then to welcome me home".

He laughed.

"We thought to kill the fatted calf", he said, "But it seems the poor beast learned of our plans and was last seen on the road to Southampton, making good speed in his escape. In the absence of his provision we have roasted two pheasants, boiled some potatoes given us by Mary Long, and prepared a variety of vegetables from the garden".

"Lead me to this repast then father", said Nell, for the week's labours at Morestead have given your daughter a fine appetite, and I am certain to do justice to your efforts".

They adjourned to the parlour, and Nell's father called for Anne to serve their meal. Anne was delighted to see Nell, and insisted upon a full description of her adventures, when she might spare the time to tell of them.

"And how have you fared in my shoes Anne", asked Nell.

"I have done my very best", said Anne, "but it is quite impossible to replace your personality about the place".

"It is only a week said Nell". "You will shine in due course .... of that I am certain. You have all been in my prayers. You will shine .... and I must soon be forgotten".

"I cannot believe such a thing Miss Nell", said Anne. "Is there no hope of you returning to us".

"Mr Barnes has the greater need", Nell said. "Surely you will not deprive him so quickly".

Anne shook her head sorrowfully.

"Then we must make the best of our condition Miss Nell", she said, "but please do not think to neglect us at the week ends".

"You need have no fear of that, at any rate", said Nell. "I shall look forward to my days at home with the greatest of longing".

Anne served the meal, which Nell, as she had promised, approached with a fine appetite.

Her father had opened a bottle of good french wine for the occasion. Nell, however, drank very little, wishing to keep a clear head for her meeting with Jack.

Her father guessed what she was about, and smiled.

"I am told by Anne that there is a black mare stabled in the mill yard", he said. "Will you think to visit that young gentleman whist you are amongst us".

Nell blushed.

"I fear I must, father", she replied. "but I doubt that he has mourned for my presence as you yourself have described. However .... I must admit that the neccessity of such a visit was praying upon my mind, and with your excusal, I shall take up my duties in that respect".

Her father laughed at her demure expression.

"With my blessing .... if not my entire approval", he said. "But there .... we have broached on these matters before, and you know that I cannot, in truth discourage you. Go forth Nell .... but guard your heart".

Nell stood, and kissed her father on the cheek.

"Thank you for my supper", she said. "It was most enjoyable".

"Let us hope that it may fortify you for the hours ahead", said her father, rising, and embracing her.

"Father ....", said Nell. "Have I not warned you before of such jests".

She left him laughing at her display of horrified indignation, collected her cloak from the entrance lobby, and set out for the mill.

....

Nell found Jack sitting at his table in the roundhouse. She had whistled, heard his response, and entered. He had just lit the first candles of the night.

He rushed to her and took her in his arms. She laid her head on his shoulder and breathed in that scent of leather, and horse, and black powder, that was so much a part of him".

"Oh Nell", he said. "I have missed you terribly. I have today counted the minutes to your return".

She kissed him on the lips, and smiled.

"And which did you truly miss the most Mr William Marseille", she asked. "Was it my inner spirit .... or was it perhaps my body. Which will you decide".

He looked at her with some surprise. Had his Nell grown so wise to the world in but five short days.

"In equal measure my Nell", he said, "But even were you to deny me your closest embrace until our marriage day, I could not forgo your company, but must needs seek it out, knowing that your presence is essential for my peace of mind".

"What is this marriage you speak of", she said. "This is news to me. Has my absence spurred you to such rashness. If so then I must propogate further of the like, in the hopes of experiencing again such admiration as has led to a proposal".

"Dearest Nell", said Jack. "Indeed your absence has prompted my words, and I determined that you would not be five minutes through the door before I sought your hand".

Nell had not initially taken his words seriously. Now she saw that he was in earnest .... and she quickly perceived her dilemma.

"Jack", she said. "Your profession, your absences, your carefree nature. What have you to offer a bride. I shall not answer immediately, but wait to enjoy every moment of your persuasions. And persuade me you must 'ere I start to consider my bridal gown".

He smiled.

"Then let that be my task", he said. "It is not an onerous one, in that you must be in my company as the persuasion proceeds. How must I begin".

Nell looked to the bed.

"Perhaps dear Sir", she said, "You might remind me of your skills in maintaining a wife, should you ever be so fortunate as to acquire the same".

....

"Jack", said Nell. "Why do you never strip me bare. I believe I could stand your gaze".

Jack, as was his want, had helped remove all but her shift. Skirts and petticoats, bodice, stockings, and shoes, but never her shift.

"It is true that I am a robber", he said, "but I am also a gentleman. And no gentleman may easily steal a lady's modesty".

"But what of her virtue", said Nell. "Will he steal that".

"Virtue is habitually judged by observers", he said. "Seldom by those who explore it's boundaries. If faithfulness is a virtue, sweet Nell, then only time will judge our value in that respect. Now take off your shift, and we will see if I can stand the effect without blushing".

Although there had been no hurry to their love making, there came that moment, as always, when Nell lay back upon her pillows, all too aware that she had discharged her duties to the young man asleep at her side, his need of her, for the ensuing hours, having been satisfied in every respect. She reflected that the circumstances of close physical relationship with a man, although natural, and indeed essential for creation, were so very different to those surrounding an intimate relationship with one of her own sex, that the two activities had little more in common than the neccessary close proximity of willing flesh. Most noticeably, thought Nell, was that the seemingly inevitable forceful, and climatic conclusion to the proceedings was entirely absent .... replaced by the gentlest transition to a peaceful contentment and loving proximity that lasted through the night, and indeed, until such time as the duties of the day might intervene to separate the participants. She lay now, wishing that the intimacy of the last hour might be continued, but had to content herself with an arm layed casually around her hips. Such was a woman's lot, she thought to herself .... whilst admitting that the experience had brought her great pleasure .... and had provided, of course, those keenly anticiparted moments of excitement, as matters reached their natural conclusion.

She was now able to answer her own question on the subject of her possible unfaithfulness to Jack. No .... she thought. My lovemaking with Jack has nothing in common with my intimate relations with Beatrice. The two are so distinctly separated that such a consideration of unfaithfulness must be quite without foundation. This still left, of course, the matters that she had discussed with the

Rev'd Johns, but Nell was young, resilient, and strong of mind. If her actions hurt nobody but herself, she argued, then surely their physical enactment could be forgiven. And, in truth, this was her personal and considered interpretation of that passage she had discussed with the good Reverend.

TWENTY NINE

Nell lay deep in thought. The candles burned low, and she needs must visit the cool outside air for her personal comfort. She returned to find Jack, with his blue riding coat about his shoulders, sitting at the table once more.

"You have risen", she said, in surprise.

"You will not be with me so long that I wish to miss the pleasure of your company by sleeping", he said. "Come Nell, sit here, and tell me of your week on the farm".

She gathered her cloak about her, and sat with him. She told him of the garden, and of Mary Long's visit. She told him of the gardener, Stubbs, and then of the young carpenter, and the closed door. She told him of her visit to the pool, and of her swimming lessons, and of the great storm, and of her lessons in Swedish. And finally she told him of her meeting with Alouette du Chambray, and of her distress, and of Giles apology.

Jacked listened carefully, and laughed as the narrative drew to a close.

"Poor Nell", he said, "Two whippings in a week. It would appear that you are want to attract such attentions".

"I am told that there was not the slightest chance of any such thing", she said.

"Indeed not", said Jack, "Or I must have words with Mr Barnes concerning your treatment. But all is well that ends well .... and your further empoyment is assured, is it not".

"It is", said Nell, and then spying Jack's account book protruding from his pocket, she remembered ....

"Jack", she said. "You have knowledge of accounting, do you not".

"I do", he said. "It has it's uses in my profession. But why do you ask".

Nell sat thinking.

"This is rather difficult for me", she said. "Giles has placed me in a position of trust. By speaking .... it might be argued that I am in breach of a confidentiality that might reasonably be expected of me in my position".

Jack nodded.

"But you are troubled by something you have discovered", he said.

Nell nodded. She remained silent.

"I am unsure of what to do for the best", she said.

"What would you do if the matter were a tribulation of spirit", said Jack.

Nell laughed.

"I would visit a close friend .... or a parson", she said.

"You would seek advice from the person you believed most likely to have the knowledge to advise you on your problem", said Jack.

"I would", said Nell.

"In that case .... you may consult with me upon this issue", said Jack. "You may make enquiry with your father upon my credentials if you wish".

"My father ....". said Nell with some puzzlement.

"I have , in the past, had the honour to advise your father on certain financial matters", said Jack, "and on one occasion was able to assist him in the hour of great need .... as you know".

Nell's face clouded.

"I do know", said Nell, "And we will forever be grateful to you".

Jack smiled.

"I did what I could", he said

"Will you promise me that what I am about to tell you will be treated with the strictest rules of confidentiality", asked Nell.

"I will", said Jack.

Nell thought again .... and drew breath to speak.

"Do you know", she said, "that I have maintained the accounts here at the tavern for the last three years".

Jack nodded.

"I do", he said. "Your father has mentioned this to me".

"The accounts of a tavern .... and those of a farm cannot be so very different", said Nell.

Jack nodded.

"Not so very different", he agreed. "There would be income on a weekly, or monthly basis to be recorded .... and then expenditures for supplies, services by trades people, and the wages of the employees. No .... not so very different".

"So would you therefore suppose, knowing as you do of my successful accounting in this tavern, that I would be able to manage the accounting for the financial activity of a farm", asked Nell.

"Assuredly", said Jack.

He looked at her closely.

"Are you then about to tell me", he said that you have viewed the accounts for Giles' farm, and that not all is as it should be".

Nell looked to the windows and the door.

"It is not so much that there are problems in the accounting", she said. "Indeed, the accounts are well kept, and the farm shows a consistent, if small, annual profit".

Jack raised his eyebrows.

"Then what ....".

"There are two issues that puzzle me", said Nell. "The first is that although the farm is mortgaged to the du Chambray family, I can find no record of the monthly payments, even though Allouette du Chambray collects them personally".

"Well", said Jack. "These payments may be recorded in a book to which you do not have access".

"That is of course possible", said Nell, "but there is a second issue which leads me to suppose that, in fact, all the account ledgers are stored together .... and it is this second issue that troubles me the most".

Jack leaned forward.

"I am intrigued, Nell", he said. "What is it that you have discovered".

"The farm accounts are kept in large ledger books", she said. "There are three of these books, the first commencing, I would suppose, when Giles took over the farm from his father. The books run chronologically, the third now having a little more than half of it's pages clear for the coming financial activity".

Jack Nodded

"But I discovered a fourth book in the cupboard", said Nell. "And it is the contents of this fourth book that trouble me because I simply cannot see what purpose the transactions recorded there might serve".

Jack listened with interest.

"The book is divided into eight sections", said Nell. "Each section is headed with a number, in some cases of two digits, some of three digits, and some of four. Under this heading is written an amount .... a capital sum it seems. And below that are written on twelve lines, twelve smaller sums, which when totalled together exceed the capital sum by five per cent. Against these recorded sums, dates are written: The twenty eighth day of each month of the calendar".

"And what do you deduce from these figures", asked Jack.

"I suppose the capital sum to be a loan taken out", said Nell. "I imagine the number of the heading to represent the lender in some way".

"Almost certainly", agreed Jack.

"And I deduce the twelve sums below to be the repayments on the loans", said Nell.

"Are the dates the actual dates on which the sums were repaid", said Jack. "Or are they perhaps the dates on which the sums are supposed to be paid".

"I am fairly certain that the dates recorded are the actual dates on which the sums were paid", said Nell. "They are written in different inks, often by different pens, and on just one occasion the date is, in fact, recorded as the first day of the following month".

"So the payments are made religiously", said Jack.

"With that one exception .... remarkably religiously", agreed Nell. "I checked carefully .... but I could find just that one exception to the rule".

Jack nodded.

"And in every case", said Nell, "as soon as the supposed loan is repaid .... twelve payments each time .... a fresh loan is taken out, and the payments begin again".

Jack shook his head.

"Does the amount borrowed vary at all", he asked.

"In all eight cases .... of the lenders, that is .... the amount increases each time a loan is renewed. In all eight cases the loan currently being repaid is the sixth loan taken out".

"What was the first sum borrowed in each case", asked Jack.

"Two hundred pounds", said Nell.

"And what sum is the subject of the current repayments", asked Jack.

"Six thousand pounds", said Nell.

"But multiplied by eight .... that is forty eight thousand pounds", said Jack. "An astonishing figure".

"In fact", said Nell, "The final monthly sum on the eight loans was paid three days ago".

"To what purpose are these borrowed sums put", asked Jack.

He closed his eyes for the purpose of mental arithmetic.

"At the rate of the current loan the interest paid is twenty four hundred pounds upon the capital. The loans must , in some way bring an income beyond that figure to make them worthwhile".

"I agree", said Nell. "But I can find no record, or indeed any practical, or physical evidence of the loans having been put to a purpose. They are taken out. They are repaid religiously, and the interest is taken from the profits of the farm".

"But that interest is two thousand four hundred pounds this year", said Jack. "Can the farm stand the amount".

"It appears so", said Nell.

"But that interest must be a terrible drain upon the annual profit figures", said Jack.

"It is", said Nell. "The farm's prosperity would be greatly improved were the sums not borrowed. I can see no reason for them".

Jack sat shaking his head.

"There is a reason Nell", he said, "Of that we can be certain. We may not be privy to it .... but that reason is there, I can assure you".

"Shall we return to our bed", asked Nell.

"We must", said Jack. "I have but a few more hours in your delightful company. Let us find good purpose for them my sweet Nell".

"Kind Sir", she said. "I shall treasure each and every moment".

THIRTY

Mr Thomas Mansell, Landlord of the Ship Inn, and his daughter, Miss Nell Mansell, attended at the Parish Church of Saint Andrews, Owslebury, on Sunday morning. Nell prayed dutifully. She enjoyed the hymns. The sermon was dreary .... and seemingly without end. She rather looked forward to her visit at Morestead Church on the coming Wedneday evening. She felt that a sermon delivered by the Rev'd Simon Johns might afford her rather more spiritual blessing than that currently being delivered by the Rev'd Mildman.

Nell and her father spoke a very few words with that good man, as they left the Church. It seemed to Nell that the Rev'd Mildman viewed her with some disapproval. Upon reflection, however, she concluded that she must be mistaken. The Rev'd Mildman was, after all, a Christian ....

Nell and her father linked arms, and strolled together, at a pleasantly leisurely pace, to their home at the Ship Inn. It was the most glorious summer morning, the unsettled weather of the last few days having succumbed to a more favourable condition.

"When will you return to Morestead, Nell", asked her father.

"I will walk back this evening", said Nell. "I would like to arrive there as my housemate, Beatrice, lights the candles for the evening. That will make for a most delightful homecoming".

"And you find your housemate to be pleasant company".

"Most pleasant company", agreed Nell. "She is thoughtful, and intelligent, with the loveliest disposition. She is teaching me her native tongue .... Swedish".

"Swedish", said her father, "I trust that you do not plan to leave us for foreign parts, Nell", he said. "That would be a grevious loss to those who love you most".

Nell laughed.

"No father", she said. "No foreign parts .... unless you count Morestead as such",

"Do they speak the same language there", he said.

Nell laughed.

"They do indeed father", she said. "I have found myself able to converse quite freely with the denizens of that parish".

They both laughed.

"Come father", said Nell. "Let us enjoy a lemonade together in the taproom .... and then I must perhaps visit at the old mill".

"Nell .... I do not know who feels your absence more. The young man .... or myself", he said.

"Then I am relieved in my mind that you at least have each other's company for your solace", she replied. "I shall not easily be forgotten while you keep company together".

Her father stopped and turned to her. He took her shoulders, and held her still.

"Nell", he said. "You can never be forgotten. That I promise you from the bottom of my heart".

They embraced fondly, and resumed their walk.

....

"A visitor for you in the parlour Mr Mansell Sir", said Anne, as they entered the taproom.

"A visitor .... and who is it, pray, Anne", he enquired.

"It is a matter of great confidentiality Sir", replied Anne. "The gentleman has asked that I do not give his name".

Tom Mansell smiled, and turned to Nell.

"It appears that you must excuse my absence for a short while, Nell", he said. "I cannot imagine what matter is so urgent that it must be discussed on a Sunday .... but hopefully the issue can be quickly resolved".

He kissed her on the forehead, and followed Anne to the parlour.

....

Nell was surprised .... but none the less delighted, when Jack suggested that they take the mare, and ride out to the woods where they had first met.

"There will be no blooms", she said.

"No bluebells, certainly", said Jack, "But it may be that we find other blooms to please our eyes".

They walked out to the mill yard, where Bess stood saddled and bridled, and quietly waiting, as was her habit.

"You do not concern yourself that we will be together in public view", said Nell. "We have habitually exercised some discretion in the matter".

Jack laughed.

"No my sweet Nell", he said. "The road to the wood is little frequented. Your good character will be preserved".

Nell shook her head in wonder .... and stood for Jack to sweep her up onto the mare's neck. She settled in her perch, and rejoiced in Jack's strong arm about her waist.

"No pistols, Jack", she said. "Where are your pistols my good Sir".

Jack laughed.

"I have no need of them on this errand", he said.

They rode happily along the old green lane that led to the woods. Jack was obviously heading towards the very spot where they had first met. He reigned Bess in some yards short of a great oak tree that stood there. He dismounted, and lifted Nell down.

"Despite the lack of bluebells", she said, "it is still a very pleasant spot".

"It is", he said.

He stood looking around, as though enjoying the aspect, then pointed to an elm in the distance.

"A Hoopoe". he said. "In the elm there .... can you see it Nell".

Nell looked at the tree he was pointing to.

She was excited. The Hoopoe, as she knew well, is an infrequent visitor to Britain's shores. It has a remarkably exotic appearance, with it's striped black and white body, pink breast, and striking crest upon it's head".

Nell searched in vain.

"I cannot see him Jack", she said.

"Then take a few steps closer", said Jack. "It may be that you are unsighted in your present position".

Nell walked a few steps closer. Again she searched the branches, but with no success.

"I cannot see it Jack. Which part ....".

She had turned .... and now she stood .... stunned into silence by what she saw.

Jack was kneeling before her, clasping a boquet of flowers in his hands.

"My dearest Miss Mansell", he said. "Will you take me as your husband".

She had said yes without the slightest thought. Without the slightest consideration as to the consequences. Without hesitation or doubt.

"I will Jack", she said.

He stood, and looked to the mare.

"Pray hold these blooms for me my good Bess", he said.

Bess took the bouquet gently into her mouth, and stood waiting patiently.

Jack embraced Nell, kissed her full on the mouth, then picked her bodily from the ground, and swung her round and round.

"Oh my sweet Nell", he said, "It seems that you have brought a highwayman to justice at last".

....

Jack delivered Nell safely to the entrance of Morestead farm as twilight fell. They stood embracing by the mare's neck. Bess nuzzled Nell's cheek.

"She tells us it is time to part, my dear Nell", said Jack.

He kissed her on her lips, mounted Bess, and was gone.

Nell entered the cottage to find Beatrice lighting the candles. She smiled.

"Welcome back my dearest Nell", said Beatrice. She came to Nell, and helped her remove her cloak and bonnet.

"I have missed you", she said simply. And she embraced her, and held her close".

Nell buried her face in the blonde ringlets she so loved. She breathed in Beatrice's clean feminine scent. She felt Beatrice's body move against her own. The sweetest, gentlest, most loving sensation, of any she had ever known.

Beatrice kissed the lobe of her ear.

"Oh my sweetest Nell", she breathed. "You light a candle within me that no breeze could extinguish".

THIRTY ONE

The morning was everything one could wish for. If absence truly makes the heart grow fonder, then the English have every reason to love the sunlight so dearly.

Nell had seen Giles and Beatrice away to Winchester. They had all that was required prepared for a delivery to the new hostelry that they had previously canvassed, and with this success fresh in his mind, Giles had located another establishment that he considered could be well worth visiting for the purpose of promoting his dairy, and it's produce.

Scarcely had Nell waved them away, when, to her surprise, the young carpenter of the week before, appeared driving a light wagonette.

"Good morning to you", said Nell. "You cannot have constructed a new door so soon. I am astonished".

The young man laughed.

"We had good fortune", he replied. "My father remembered that there was, in our store, a door and frame already completed, the order for it having been cancelled. We checked the measurements, and to our surprise, discovered that, with the slightest of modifications, it would fit the bill perfectly. And it is a handsome door to boot. You will be well pleased with it, I'm certain".

Nell watched as he and his helper lifted the door and frame from the rear of their transport, and laid it upon a pair of trestles, ready for work to commence.

"Now", said the young man, choosing a hammer and bolstered chisel from his tool box. "Let us open up the doorway that was closed".

Nell saw the first bricks come out, but such was the noise and dust, that she decided upon a visit to the poultry. It was, in any case, well and truly time that she reminded the hens of their forthcoming duties. Their time of relaxation in the sun was soon to be over.

The poultry having been given the benefit of her instruction, Nell went next to the kitchen garden. The transformation here was a joy to behold. All the former signs of dereliction had vanished. The trees were pruned, the fruit cages cleared and repaired, the ground ploughed and harrowed .... and the plants arrived from the Hall at Marwell.

"I am quite delighted Mr Stubbs", she said. "The improvement is a marvel".

Stubbs straightened from his labours. He was planting runner beans in the rich tilled soil. He looked around the plot, and smiled at her.

"Thank you Ma'am", he said. "I will admit that we have got on better than I could have imagined. The pony plough and harrow were a great help with the soil, and the two lads I was able to procure, worked wonders with the fruit cages".

"And the fruit trees look wonderful", said Nell.

"Ah", said Stubbs. "I do enjoy pruning. It is a satisfying occupation, once one has learned the art. And though I says it, as shouldn't, I reckon as you'll be pleased with the result".

"I'm certain that we will, Mr Stubbs", said Nell. "May I offer you a cool lemonade".

"Well Ma'am", said Stubbs, "I'd be a foolish man to say no to such an offer on a warm morning. Thank you kindly Ma'am".

Nell went to fetch the lemonade, providing the young carpenter with the same, whilst she was in the kitchen.

He sipped gratefully.

"As you can see Miss", he said. Just a few more bricks to remove. I'll clean up the opening, and then in goes the frame".

He looked at the sun.

"If all goes well", he said, "I might have the door in place by mid afternoon".

"Then I must leave you to concentrate on the task in hand", said Nell, and, having delivered the lemonade to the garden, went off to the dairy, where she was immediately co-opted into the butter making. This was new to her .... but the two dairy maids who normally assisted Beatrice were forthcoming with instruction, and praise for her efforts, and she much enjoyed the time spent in their company. They seemed happy and relaxed, freed, as Nell supposed, from the threat of being made to stand in the corner to reflect upon their wrong-doings.

It was well past three in the afternoon before Nell could return to her kitchen. She found the young craftsman putting the final touches to the door. He showed her the results of his labours. Nell went outside, and lifted the latch.

"A shame there is no one to carry you over the threshold", he said .... and then laughed at her shocked expression.

"I do apologise Miss", he said. "It is the normal carpenter's quip on such an occasion".

"Perhaps you might carry me", said Nell,

It was the carpenters turn to be embarassed.

"Much though I would love to Miss", he said, "I fear that my good wife might have something to say about the matter".

They both laughed.

Nell made her first entrance through a door unused for many years, and then stood looking around her.

"Could I possibly prevail upon you to help me move some of the furniture into this newly useful room", she said. "I fear that the great dresser will defeat us, but some of the smaller pieces might be manageable".

"Where would you like the dresser", asked the young man.

"Well, it is in the old kitchen, and I would like it to be moved to the new", said Nell.

"Then we shall move it", said the carpenter, and he brought four wooden rollers from his tool box. To Nell's astonishment the dresser stood in it's new position within five minutes.

"You could move the Earth with a good set of rollers", said the craftsman, smiling at her pleasure in the accomplishment.

"Might we move the bureau desk to occupy the position left vacant by the movement of the dresser", she asked.

Again the move was quickly done.

The young man stood looking at the bureau,

"A fine piece of oak furniture", he said. "Made locally, by the style of it. Have you found a secret drawer in it yet Miss".

"A secret drawer", said Nell. "That sounds fascinating. Is it really likely to have such a fitment, do you think".

"Almost certainly", said the carpenter. "Perhaps "secret" is not the correct word .... but a concealed drawer or compartment for storing small items, out of harms way, is commonly a part of these pieces of furniture".

"Can you show me where such a thing might be located", said Nell.

The young man smiled, and went to his tool box for a measuring rod. He showed Nell how to measure the internal depth of the cubby holes, in the upper section of the piece, and then to compare those measurements with the external depth of what he referred to as the "carcass". To his surprise the measurements were all the same.

"Nothing to be found there", he said.

He turned his attention to the drawers in the lower half of the piece, again comparing internal measurements with external. He sat back on his heels with a puzzled expression on his countenance.

"Nothing", he said. "This is very odd, very unusual. These bureaux seldom lack their concealed compartments. And although he spent another ten minutes in his examination .... he eventually admitted defeat.

"If it is there Miss", he said. "The man who built it was a master of his craft. He has beaten us to be sure".

"Is it not simply that this piece of furniture was built without", asked Nell.

The carpenter stood, and began to gather his tools together.

"It is possible Miss", he said. "Possible .... and yet I still feel the builder has outwitted us".

He laughed.

"I must away", he said.

Leaving his tool box to be collected later in the day, by the wagonette, he bade Nell farewell, and set off for his home. Nell admired the new door, and, quite unneccessarily, traversed it's now open way a number of times to test it's efficiency.

She sat on a chair, and looked at the Bureau.

"Do you hold a secret, Mr Bureau", she said to herself.

She decided upon a clearance of the drawers, sorting the papers they contained into those that should be retained, those that could be burned, and those of which she was uncertain .... intending to show them to Giles, that he might decide their fate.

And it was whilst she was engaged in this absorbing task, that the desk gave up it's secret. The top left hand drawer was a full inch shallower than it's fellow on the right. Nell examined the drawer closely. She quickly discovered that the back of the drawer could be slid upwards, allowing the false bottom to slide out. She had the drawer inverted as she made this discovery. She slid out the false base .... and a paper fell to the floor.

Placing the dismantled drawer to one side, Nell picked up the paper, unfolded it, and examined it's contents.

She sank back to her seat. She had seen a similar document only recently.

She looked in disbelief at the words.

In her hand she held a certificate of marriage issued in London. A certificate of marriage between Mr Giles Barnes .... and Miss Alouette, Sophia, Marie, du Chambray. It was dated some three years previously.

Nell sat shaking her head in puzzlement.

THIRTY TWO

Jack Marseille sat in the taproom of the Ship Inn, at Owslebury, absorbed in a game of cribbage with old John Boyes. The landlord placed two tankards of ale before them. He stood watching the game for a few minutes, until, as is a landlords lot in life, he was called away to his barrels.

Jack and Nell had made public the news of their engagement to be married, and Jack had yet to purchase a drink that evening, his tankard replenished the moment he had emptied it. He had been the subject of much curiosity, and no little banter. In truth, the regular customers of the tavern had been uncertain as to how they might view the news of this forthcoming marriage, but they looked to Nell's father for their guidance, and perceiving that he seemed happy and contented with the affair, they fell into line with praise and congratulations .... and a steady supply of ale .... for the young man brave enough to suppose that he might tame their dear Nell.

The first hour of the evening had certainly been a lively one for Jack .... but things had now quietened. John Boyes had come in rather later than was normal. He had missed the earlier ribaldry, but added his own congratulations, and he and Jack were soon absorbed in their normal pastime. The age old game of cribbage.

The old man seemed in excellent spirits,

"Jack", he said. "It seems today that we have both set to a fair wind for our futures".

"Are you to marry then John", Jack asked him, smiling.

The old man slapped his knee and laughed heartily.

"No Jack", he said. "That is a young man's pursuit. I have my financial future in mind, and have today made an investment that will see me secured for my remaining years".

"I trust that you have invested wisely with those of good repute", said Jack.

"I have invested with the party on several previous occasions", said John. "My returns have been made on the date set for their payment, and accurate to the last penny, on every occasion. I have no worries as to the integrity of my investment".

"Is the sum involved a largish one", asked Jack.

"It is", said the old farmer. "My life savings .... but I shall see it back over the coming years with a handsome return for my pains".

"I wish you all the best for your future", said Jack. "I'm confident that you are a good enough judge of human nature to assess any venture accurately, 'ere you take it up".

"I believe I am", said John. "I started as a boy behind the plough, and rose to own two farms. There were difficult times .... but I always seemed, with the Good Lord's help, to see my way through".

Jack sat staring at him.

"A penny for your thoughts young Jack", said the old man. "Another penny will not hurt me after this days financial investment".

"I apologise to you for my distraction", said Jack. "I did not know that you owned two farms John. Where then is the second".

The old farmer looked up from the game.

"It is perhaps not common knowledge", he said, "But I own Morestead farm ....".

"Morestead farm", said Jack, "but that surely is the farm of Mr Giles Barnes .... having inherited the responsibility from his father".

"He inherited the responsibility to be sure", said John Boyes, "But I bought the farm from his father when that good man, through events for which he was not entirely to blame, was left without the means to continue".

Jack again sat silently

"Then Giles has no equity in the farm at all", he asked.

"None whatsoever", replied John. "He may own the clothes he stands up in .... but I own the rest ....".

At this moment they were disturbed by an altercation at the counter.

"But Tom", a young man cried. "You have extended me credit on several previous occasions. Have I not always paid you back".

"You have indeed Paul", said the landlord, "And aware, as I am, that the amount has increased upon each occasion, I invoke my right to exercise caution".

"But ....".

Tom Mansell held up his hand.

"You must understand Paul", he said. "The amounts you have previously borrowed have been such that they were well worth paying back. But I am reluctant, indeed I would be foolish, to lend an amount that would be well worth not paying back".

He had placed great emphasis on the word "not".

The young man, Paul, stood staring at him. Jack expected him to remonstrate, but he turned on his heel and left the tap room. The landlord watched him go.

"Oh dear", he said. "I have lost a customer .... but perhaps I have gained the astonished respect of that young man".

Jack sat transfixed, the puzzle that Nell had set him having been suddenly laid open to startling examination. He looked at his companion, with apprehension forming in his mind at a quite alarming rate. There was a question that he wished to ask John Boyes. A question of paramount importance for that good farmer's future. But he feared to ask it. Suppose he were wrong. He dare not set the old man's mind alight with fears that might have absolutely no foundation.

He sat staring. The tally board in the corner by the barrels held his gaze .... with it's numbers indicating the individual purchasers .... and the quarts they had purchased that evening. Jack knew it was the custom of the house to exercise discretion with this board. A man's name was listed by numbers, the digits representing the place in the alphabet of that man's initials. A simple system .... but discreet.

Jack rose suddenly.

"You must excuse me John", he said. "I have greatly enjoyed our game, but the hour is late, and I have one more appointment to keep tonight".

The old man laughed.

"Ah", he said, "What it is to be young .... with a damsel to woo".

He stood, and shook Jack's hand.

"Well met young Jack", he said. "Well met indeed".

....

Old John Boyes had been, at least, partially correct. Jack was intent upon a visit to his fiancee .... with very great haste. But not to woo that young lady .... not tonight.

He returned to the Mill, saddled his mare, and rode out for Morestead. Within twenty minutes he was in the farm yard. The under carter came out to greet him.

"My good man", said Jack. "I have urgent business with Miss Nell Mansell. Can you tell me where she might be found".

The carter smiled.

"Miss Mansell and Miss Beatrice have walked up to the church", he said.

"To a service", said Jack, in surprise.

"I would hardly imagine so Sir", said the man."Not on a Monday at any rate".

Jack thanked him .... and turned the mare towards the church.

....

The Rev'd Johns had contrived another scheme to bring the young people of his parish to their Church. He had thought to form a choir, and had visited the farm that afternoon to cajole Nell, and then Beatrice, and then the two dairy maids, to visit the church that evening for an hour, that he might assess their voices for this new scheme. The four of them were rather taken with the idea of standing at the front of a service to lead the hymns and agreed quite readily to a meeting at the Church after their supper had been eaten. Nell, certainly was delighted to have the offer of such a distraction. Her discovery of the concealed marriage cerificate troubled her greatly. She could see no reason for such a deception, and felt that she must consult with Jack, when she next had opportunity.

The four young women from Morestead farm arrived at the Church to discover that their counterparts from another nearby farm had been similarly persuaded. It was a most happy gathering, and the Rev'd Johns seemed perfectly assured in his management of these eight young members of the gentler sex.

The practise had gone well, the Rev'd Johns providing music from a small and portable organ which he had brought to Morestead amongst his possessions. Everybody had enjoyed singing the lively hymns he had suggested, he had thought to serve them lemonade and biscuits in the meeting room afterwards, and it was almost dark before the young women started to depart for their homes.

"Could I trouble you for a private word Miss Mansell", the Rev'd Johns asked her quietly, as she and Beatrice stood in the doorway.

Nell looked to her friend.

"I will walk on ahead and light the candles", said Beatrice.

"Nell", said the Rev'd Johns, when they were alone. "On the passage that we discussed".

Nell nodded.

"You asked if our Saviour forgave a certain young woman".

"Upon reflection, I feel that He did", she said. "Have you yourself had further thoughts on the matter".

The Rev'd Johns nodded.

"Only this", he said. "That whilst forgiveness might be sought from those that we have sinned against, it is sometimes most difficult of all to forgive ones self".

Nell thought.

"That is true", she said. "Could that young woman forgive herself. And that surely must depend upon the attitude of those around her .... those she loves most".

She bade the Rev'd a good night, and turned, and walked away.

....

Nell was astonished to find Jack waiting for her at the base of the steps that led down into the road.

"Jack", she said, "What brings you here at such late hours".

He embraced her .... but his mind was clearly elsewhere.

"Nell", he said. "There is great urgency to this question. Can you recall the numbers that headed the pages in the ledger book of loans. Can there have been the number one, nought, two amongst the eight you mentioned".

Nell thought.

"I cannot be certain Jack", she said. "Why such a question. Have you developed a theory to explain the loans",

"I would be a happier man if I could say no", answered Jack.

He scooped Nell up to her habitual seat on the mare's neck, and rode for the farm.

THIRTY THREE

The ride to the farm was but a short one. They dismounted at the farmhouse door, alarmed to find all in darkness.

Jack shook his head, his fears growing in his mind.

He tethered Bess whilst Nell entered the old kitchen, and sought illumination. The fire was alight in the hearth, and she was able to quickly light two candles. She gasped in horror at the scene around her. The room was in chaos. The bureau had been emptied. The ashes in the hearth showed the fate of the papers it had recently held. The drawer that had contained the secret compartment lay smashed on the floor.

"The marriage certificate has been taken", cried Nell.

"Of what certificate do you speak, Nell", asked Jack.

"Giles Barnes and Alouette du Chambray are husband and wife", said Nell. "They were married in London three years ago".

The news seemed to come as no surprise to Jack.

"The ledger that recorded the loans", he said. "Where was it kept, Nell".

Nell rushed to the cupboard and wrenched open the doors. It was empty. All four books had gone.

"The fire", said Jack.

He strode to it, and cried out to her.

"Is this the book", he said.

Only the upper half of the small ledger had survived the flames, the lower half being quite burned away. Jack brushed away the ash and dust, and they looked at the page headings. On page four they found what Jack had not wished to find. The page was headed with "one, nought, two".

"One, nought being ten", said Jack. "The tenth letter of the alphabet is J. The two is the second letter, B. The number is the page heading for John Boyes".

Nell had looked at another heading.

"Ten, and twelve", she said. "That might be Joshua Long. My friend Mary Long's father. I wonder if we can decipher the other six headings".

"There is no time", said Jack. "The fire has burned, and the birds are flown".

"Why flown", said Nell. "What does all this mean Jack".

"The loans were made for the purpose of creating a line of credit, a line of good faith and good will", said Jack. "They were religiously repaid that the lender would issue further credit without fear of default. The amounts were increased with each successive loan".

He thought.

"Has Giles been much absent these last few days". he asked.

"He has", said Nell.

"Then assuming that the loan amount was increased to eight thousand pounds each, from the normal eight lenders, Giles could be in current posession of some sixty four thousand pounds, Nell", he said. "And that is an amount well worth not paying back".

"But his ties to the farm", said Nell, scarce able to believe that which Jack had put before her.

"He has no ties", said Jack. "John Boyes owns the farm. He bought it from Giles' father. John told me as much scarce an hour since, and he told me of an investment he had made today to provide for his old age. Giles has, if I am correct, some eight thousand pounds taken from John Boyes. That sum represents the old man's life savings".

"But the farm is mortgaged to the du Chambray family", said Nell. John Boyes cannot own it".

"I suspect that tale has it's origins in Giles' fertile imagination", said Jack. "It gave him some degree of status in his activities to be "owner" of Morestead farm. John Boyes may have seen little harm in his so claiming .... whilst he managed the farm properly".

Nell shook her head.

"And as for Alouette du Chambray", he said. "I have met with many great ladies in my past activities. They do not normally find it pleasant to act as Mlle. Chambray acted towards you. Kindness and graciousness is more their natural way, believe me Nell".

"Then what must we do Jack", Nell said. "Giles cannot have flown so very far, if it was indeed he who cleared the papers, and lit the fire".

Jack looked around him.

"That is true Nell", he said. "He might yet be caught, but in which direction must we ride".

"If Alouette is part of this deception", said Nell, "Then she will wait for Giles at the coaching Inn at Whiteflood. If they intend to flee to France, they will take the Portsmouth road from there. It might be that they will not leave until daylight".

"It is possible", said Jack. "That must be our first place of enquiry in any event. If they are not there .... it may be that we can gather news of their movements".

....

Captain Ebineezer Mears surveyed his platoon with a growing feeling that this night patrol would be frought with difficulty. The eight young men in their Militia uniforms were all very young. Very young .... and very enthusiastic. And as Captain Mears was well aware, there is nothing more to be feared in a very young Militia man, than a surfeit of enthusiasm. Enthusiasm invariably ends in somebody getting hurt. Captain Mears did not wish to see his young men hurt. He certainly did not wish to be hurt himself.

Tonight he had been ordered to take his platoon on a patrol of the old Portsmouth to Winchester road: that their presence might deter highwaymen. This was supposedly a popular haunt for these gentlemen of the road. Captain Mears had never seen a highwayman. He did not wish to see one tonight. A nice peaceful march out in the moonlight, from their makeshift barracks at Droxford, a nice peaceful march back, as the new day dawned, and breakfast in the tap room of the White Horse Tavern. That was his plan. And with a platoon of older and more experienced men, there was every chance that he, as a Militia Captain, could go about his business, that those gentlemen of the road, the highwaymen, might go about their business, and, with good fortune, the Portsmouth road might prove to be quite long enough, that neither party need interfere unduly with the business of the other.

He surveyed his troups. The oldest of them might just have reached his eighteenth year. He shuddered.

"Attention", he called.

The young men brought their arms to their shoulders. They were all supplied with new equipment for this type of patrol work. Each carried a flintlock carbine. The gun was based on that military favourite, the "Brown Bess" musket .... but much shortened, and somewhat lighter in the stock.

Captain Mears sighed. He disliked guns intensely. Guns resulted in injuries. He was a career Militia man. The life suited him. And by life, he meant just that. Dying for King and country was in no way part of his personal plans.

Regulations decreed that for this type of patrol, when immediate and unexpected action might well be called for, they must march with fully loaded weapons. This was plainly sensible from a militaristic viewpoint. But with eight young men in their teens under his care, Captain Mears did not feel it to be sensible in any way at all. In his experience, those who fired a gun could invariably be expected to be fired upon in return .... and that is how people got hurt.

He was not a happy man as he led his patrol out of Droxford, and headed for the Portsmouth road.

....

"I insist on accompanying you Jack", said Nell.

He looked down at her from the saddle.

"I can ride more swiftly alone Nell". he said.

"I have to go with you Jack", she replied. "I have business with Giles Barnes".

"Is there another riding horse here that we might saddle for you", he asked.

Bess stirred impatiently.

"None", she said. "Take me with you please".

Exasperated, he swung her up before him. Bess was away almost before he had touched her flanks. Jack held Nell back against his chest. They turned right onto the Corhampton road, Jack doing his best to hold his mare back, lest she exhaust herself too soon. Up over the hill, down into Owslebury bottom, and then the long long climb to Greenhill. Bess fell into a steadier pace. Jack relaxed a little. It might be that they need travel no further than Whiteflood and it's coaching inn.

Some thirty minutes later Nell held Bess's head in the yard of "The Flood". Jack had gone to the ostler to seek news. He was back with Nell in minutes.

"We have missed them by five minutes", he said. "Alouette spent the day here waiting for Giles to join her. They have travelled on in her coach. The ostler is saddling Giles' mount for you as we speak".

"That his own mount should lead to his downfall would be poetic justice indeed", said Nell.

The ostler appeared with a mare that Nell immediately recognised as one belonging to Giles. Jack gave the ostler a half guinea, and they were off along the road to Portsmouth.

"But which route will they take", shouted Nell. "They could turn for Bishops Waltham, and then on for Wickham, or will they stay on this road, and turn for Droxford at Corhampton".

"With the carriage the ostler described", said Jack, "they will continue on this road and turn for Droxford. It would be the faster way, as the route is better maintained than the one to Bishops Waltham".

They encouraged the horses to give their best, and some twenty minutes later Jack raised his arm signalling to Nell that they should slow. On the far side of the valley, some half a mile ahead, they could see the lights of a carriage moving up the hill.

"Ten minutes, and we have them", said Jack. He beckoned her closer. "I will overhaul them, turn, and bring the carriage to a standstill", he said.

Nell nodded.

"Stay back initially", said Jack. "I will beckon you closer when I have gauged their mood. When you saw the carriage in the farm yard, did you see a blunderbuss or pistols mounted for the driver or footman".

"None", said Nell.

"The ostler said the same", said Jack. "It may be that we can end this business peacefully .... perhaps even persuade Giles Barnes to return the monies himself".

"It was for that reason that I insisted upon joining you", said Nell. "He has known me since we attended the village school together. It might be that he will listen to my persuasion".

Jack nodded.

"On with the business then", he said, and touched his mare's flanks. Nell followed.

They came up behind the coach, on a short straight section of the road.
Jack paced Bess parallel with the lead horse, grabbed it's halter, and rode the vehicle to a stand still. Nell hung back, waiting for his signal. There was an altercation, shouting, cries from Alouette. Jack stood on the foot board of the coach looking within. The driver and footman seemed frozen in their seats.

And then Nell saw a group of men coming around the bend that lay ahead of them. They were marching in an orderly rank, and she recognised them as Militia men.

She saw the coach driver leap from his seat, and run towards them,

"Highwaymen", he shouted, "Highwaymen".

Nell rode forwards to assist Jack. She saw the footman produce a long coaching pistol. He seemed not to aim it, but simply discharged it into the air as, Nell supposed, a warning of trouble to the Militia.

She reached Jack as the Militia men broke into a run. The footman brought out the second pistol of his pair.

"Not needed", shouted Jack. "Wait for the Militia to come up".

The footman took no heed. He discharged the piece as Jack struck his arm away. Nell saw one of the Militia raise his weapon.

"No", she shouted. "All is well. Do not fire upon us".

And she rode in front of Jack.

The bullet took her in the back. She crumpled from her mount. Jack was with her almost before she had fallen from the saddle. He tore a cushion from the carriage's interior, and laid her head upon it.

She looked up at him.

"Jack", she said. "I believe I am struck down. Will you help me".

There was blood on her breath as she spoke.

"Hush dear Nell", he said. "You must lay your head back upon this cushion, and I will examine your wounds".

She sighed, and closed her eyes. Jack began to unfasten her bodice. She shook her head.

"Jack", she said, "Do you seek to disrobe me in public view".

"Hush Nell", he said. "I need to examine your wounds".

He re-arranged her cloak that it might serve to preserve her modesty, then gently removed her bodice. He slipped his hand beneath her shoulder, his fingers seeking the wound. He drew his hand back. It was soaked in blood. Although he searched, he could find no exit wound. The bullet was lodged deep inside her.

"Jack", she said. "Will you hold me close".

He pressed his face to her cheek and held her.

"That is well Jack", she said. "You must not be alarmed for me .... after all .... it does not hurt me so very much".

And she closed her eyes, and lay back upon the cushion.

The Militia Captain came up. Jack produced a token from his pocket. The Captain stared at it. His face blanched.

"Take the brown mare", said Jack, "and ride for a physician. Ride like the wind. You have struck down an agent of His Majesty".

The man stared at him.

"Go", said Jack, "and ride as you've never ridden before".

The man mounted, and was gone into the night. Jack turned his attention back to Nell.

"Nell", he said. "They have ridden for a physician. Be still now".

"I fear it will be too late", she said. And she smiled at Jack. And then she lay still, with her head upon the cushion.

THIRTY FOUR

Nell opened her eyes. She was standing in bright sunlight .... in a cornfield. The breeze ruffled her hair, and all around her a gently swaying crop of oats stretched away into the distance. Far away, a figure stood by the fence, looking out over the crop. Nell started towards him, brushing her hands over the heads of the oats, as she walked. She glanced behind her, puzzled to notice that her passage left no trace amongst the stems.

A young man stood there, as though waiting for her. He smiled as she approached.

"Welcome Nell", he said, and held out his hand to her.

"How do you know me", she asked.

"It is my business to know all on my master's farm", he said.

"Are you the farmer's son then", she asked.

He laughed.

"No Nell", he said. "I am the shepherd. I tend the flocks .... but occasionally I walk up to these fields to view the harvest".

They stood looking out over the golden field of oats, the swollen heads swaying in the breeze.

"It will be a wonderful harvest", said Nell, who still held his hand.

The shepherd sighed.

"It will be a wonderful harvest", he said, "But the harvest is great, and those who must gather it are so few. Have you come to help gather the harvest Nell".

She shook her head.

"I am the manager for a farm", she said .... and she stood reflecting, ".... but if my help is needed .... then yes, I will help to gather in the harvest".

"We must all help to gather in when the crop is so great", he said. "Come now Nell, and let us meet the master of this farm, that you might recognise him".

He led her to a gate, and allowed her through into a meadow lush with grass. A milk herd surveyed them from beneath a stand of beech trees.

They walked hand in hand down the hill, until the farm yard came into sight. It seemed strangely familiar to Nell.

The shepherd stopped.

"You must go on alone", he said, "But do not be alarmed. Your heart's desires await you".

He took Nell's hands and drew her to him, and placed a kiss on her forehead.

"Go forth Nell", he said.

She moved away .... and then turned. She closed her eyes .... and tried to remember the question that she must ask.

"Am I forgiven", she said.

He smiled at her.

"You are forgiven", he said.

She started down the hill, and he watched her go, and he looked back to the harvest, and out over the meadows, and He smiled.

And as she neared the farm yard, she saw the farmer waiting for her.

And as she walked, she saw a bridal gown, and a village church, and a throng of local people. She saw a decorated cart, and heard Church bells, and she saw herself carried across a threshold. She saw herself as the head of a thriving enterprise. The dairy to run. Poultry to manage. Summer in the cornfields. Harvest homes, and Christmas gatherings. She came to the gate, and found it open, and she went joyfully through it, and she found children about her skirts.

The farmer welcomed her.

"Am I come home", she said.

"Nell, you are come home", he replied.

And he took her arm in his own, and led her to the farmhouse, and a young woman in the garb of a dairy maid came out to greet them. And she came to Nell, and kissed her, and held her close.

Nell turned, and looked to the farmer.

He smiled.

"Where there is love, there can be no sin", he said. And he took their hands and joined them, and sent them to the dairy, that the milk might be cooled, and the butter might be churned, and the cheese might be made.

And they went there, and the children thronged about their skirts.

THE END

A MEADOW RICH WITH BUTTERFLIES

The car pulled onto a gravel area by the roadside.

"Here we are", said Cathy. "This must be our last visit of the day, I'm afraid. Your mother is collecting you after supper, so we need to get home a little earlier than normal".

She looked at her granddaughters fondly. It had been such a wonderful pleasure to have them stay for the week. They were growing up so quickly. This might be the last time that "Grams" was asked to "mind the children".

Not that they needed much minding. When her daughter Alison had first brought her fiance, Andrew, home, all those years ago, Cathy had looked at him and thought: He will be a wonderful husband .... and a wonderful father. And he had been both.

If somebody were kind enough to mention to Andrew and Alison, that their daughters were becoming very lovely young ladies, Andrew would smile, and rub his chin thoughtfully, and say:

"Do you know .... I believe they are. I blame the parents myself".

It always made Cathy smile. And yes .... Andrew and Alison quite deserved the "blame" for Aurora, and her younger sister Emma.

She looked at them now. Plainly sisters, but so very very different. The athletic Aurora was the epitome of an enthusiastic English schoolgirl. Her seeming inexhaustible energy made her excel at any sport she tried. Tennis, netball, swimming, hockey .... anything, in fact, that would keep those young latch, constant motion. Even at this moment, she was dressed in a fleece. cream pleated tennis skirt .... as though to be immediately ready should the opportunity arise.

Her sister, on the other hand, was the more studious of the, but she really enough to take part in sports at school, to be part of hnentary playing on preferred to have a book in her hand, or a You tub\`d biology, but there was little her Samsung tablet. Her great passions were hist\`ught her eye. she was not interested in, once the subect ha\`

./1

"What are you going to show us now, Grams", said Emma. "There doesn't seem to be much to look at just here".

They looked out over a grass meadow that gently sloped away behind them. It took the form of a shallow valley. The grass was a lush green, even after the draught of the last few weeks. There were wild flowers in the grass, and they could see butterflies wherever they looked.

"Do you see that copse of trees further down the valley", asked Cathy. "That's where we're going".

"Why", asked Aurora.

"Be patient Aurora", said Emma. "Grams will tell us when we get there .... won't you, Grams", she added.

"Grams" nodded.

"When we get there", she said. "And not a moment before".

They climbed from the car and Cathy locked it. They slipped between the wooden rails of the fence, and started across the meadow.

"It's about a quarter of a mile from here to the edge of the copse", said Cathy, ".... and I have a five pound note for the first of you to run to the edge of the trees and back to me".

"That's just not fair Grams", said Emma. "Aurora is going to win easily. She's much more athletic than I am .... and she has a tennis skirt on. I'm wearing my best ⌐ns".

Smiled at her .... and then Emma realised her grandmother's purpose. The ⌐ give some exercise to her sister Aurora's ever restless limbs.

"Alright G⌐

"Is that Ok with y⌐aid, "But can I have a fifty yard start".

Aurora nodded.   ⌐", asked her grandmother.

"You could take your jeans off", Emm, she said, smiling.

"I am not going to be seen running across meadows in my pants", said Emma. "No way, Aurora".

Cathy laughed.

"A fifty yard start it is then", she said. "Off you go then, Emma".

She and Aurora stood and watched, waiting for Emma to walk on for fifty yards.

"We said fifty yards .... not a hundred", Aurora called, when she thought Emma had gone quite far enough.

Emma stopped and waved.

"Ready", she called.

"On the count of three then .... ". Cathy raised her arm, holding her handerchief as a makeshift starter's flag.

"Are you ready Aurora", she asked.

"Ready, Grams".

Cathy dropped her flag, and stood to watch as both girls sprinted away, astonished at the clouds of butterflies disturbed by their passage.

The race was not, after all, quite such a certainty. Emma had a plan for the five pounds prize money .... which gave her an incentive to make that little extra effort. Aurora, on the other hand, had perhaps not quite realised that fifty yards was a fair distance to be made up, before the contest could begin in earnest.

Some fifty yards from "Grams", on the return leg, Aurora really had the race won, but Emma put on an heroic final spurt for the finish line. Whether it would have been sufficient, we shall never know, because, at that moment, Aurora stumbled in a rut concealed in the grass. She fell, was soon up again, with no harm done, but the stumble had cost her the race .... and the five pounds.

"Are you alright Aurora", asked her grandmother, as the loser ran up, panting.

Aurora laughed.

"Apart from grass stains on my new tennis skirt, I'm fine Grams", she said. She examined the stains on her cream pleats.

"Don't worry, I have some stain remover", said her grandmother.

"Oh .... I'm not worried", said Aurora. "Tennis skirts always get grass stained. I fall over all the time, chasing base line shots".

She turned to her sister.

"Well done Emma", she said. "That was a lot closer than I thought it would be. You would have won if you'd taken those jeans off".

Emma rolled her eyes skywards.

By this time they were coming up to the edge of the copse. Cathy led them around the outkirts, until she found a pathway that would take them into the trees.

A few minutes later she brought them out onto a grassy bank surrounding a pool. The girls stood staring in astonishment.

"It's just so beautiful", said Emma, "It's amazing".

"I wish I'd brought a swimming costume", said Aurora, looking at the water.

"You could swim in your bra and pants", said Emma, laughing.

"Oh very quick Emma", said Aurora. "Touché indeed".

She looked at water.

"But I suppose I could", she said. "Would you mind awfully, Grams".

Her grandmother shook her head.

"I'm sorry to say no, Aurora, but bathing here is very strictly forbidden", she said.

"Why", asked Emma.

"The water is extremely cold", said Cathy. "It comes from a natural spring, in the centre of the pool. It is cold enough to rob you of your breath. The pool is also very deep .... perhaps a hundred feet. It is thought originally to have been created by early men mining for flints. They had reached that depth .... when they hit the spring. There is a narrow shallows around the circumference of the pool, but it drops without warning, almost sheer to the bottom. It is a very dangerous place to bathe".

Aurora shook her head.

"And yet it looks so lovely", she said.

"It does indeed", said Cathy, "But come around to the other side, and I will show you something".

She led her granddaughters to a sunlit area on the other side of the water. She searched around the bushes at it's edge.

"Here", she said.

She parted the greenery to reveal a small headstone. Although covered in lichens, the inscription was just discernible.

"Can you read what it says, Emma", asked Cathy.

Aurora looked on in interest, as her sister rubbed the face of the stone with her palm, and knelt down to study the words she had revealed.

"I can see a date at the bottom", she said. She traced her finger along the elegantly carved figures.

"It's 1720", she said. " .... and there are two names .... I think".

She studied them carefully, rubbing away lichen with her finger tips.

"Beatrice Hedlund .... and Nell Manfell", she said.

Cathy smiled at her.

"Nell Mansell", she said. "The letter S was written as an F in those days".

"Who were they", said Aurora.

"They were two girls, only a little older than yourselves", said Cathy. "One very hot afternoon, they came here from the farm at Morestead to bathe. Beatrice was an experienced swimmer, but the coldness of the water took her by surprise. Her limbs cramped, and she had gone beyond the shallows. She cried out in fear, and poor

Nell tried to help her. She could not swim .... but she went to her friend's aid".

Cathy fell silent, staring at the water.

"And they both perished ....", said Emma.

"I'm afraid that they did", said her grandmother.

"Are the bodies buried here", asked Aurora.

"No", said Cathy. "They were buried, side by side, in the church yard at Morestead. The stone here was erected to mark the spot .... and to act as a warning to others".

"That's so sad", said Emma. "Were they the farmer's daughters".

"No", said Cathy. "Nell Mansell had started work at the farm that very morning. She was the daughter of a Tom Mansell, the landlord of the Ship Inn at Owslebury. Beatrice Hedlund was from Sweden. She was the head dairy maid at the farm.

They all stood staring at the stone. The area shaded suddenly as a cloud passed over the sun. A light wind ruffled the surface of the pool.

Cathy and Aurora started away, but Emma stayed kneeling at the stone. She placed her hands upon it .... and thought of her own very very special friend at school .... dearest Eleanor. Her finger tips sought the locket, on it's chain around her neck.

"Nell and Beatrice", she said softly. "Why did you come here that afternoon. Why did you come here .... were you lovers perhaps .... were you so very much in love".

And she began to cry. And then she stood and followed her Sister and her grandmother .... away from the pool, and away from the copse. Towards the car .... and home .... across a meadow. A meadow rich with butterflies.

THE END

(or perhaps a beginning ....)